RUNNING

DIFFICULTY AT THE BEGINNING

BOOK ONE

Keith Maillard

BRINDLE
& GLASS

Library and Archives Canada Cataloguing in Publication
Maillard, Keith, 1942-
Difficulty at the beginning / Keith Maillard.

Contents: bk. 1. Running — bk. 2. Morgantown —
bk. 3. Lyndon Johnson and the majorettes — bk. 4. Looking good.
ISBN 1-897142-06-4 (bk. 1).—ISBN 1-897142-07-2 (bk. 2).—
ISBN 1-897142-08-0 (bk. 3).—ISBN 1-897142-09-9 (bk. 4)

I. Title.

PS8576.A49D54 2005   C813/.54   C2005-903472-6

Cover image: istockphoto.com
Author photo: Mary Maillard

Acknowledgements: The story of John's race at Harrod (pp. 75–81) originally appeared in considerably different form in *Fusion* (No. 26, July 1972; Boston, MA) in an article entitled "Grown Up Absurd." The story of John's race with Cassandra (pp. 141–48) first appeared, in a slightly different form, in *The Malahat Review* (No. 50, April 1979; Victoria, BC) under the title of "Running: The Fifties." On page 34, John's memory is playing tricks on him, and he doesn't remember the song "Stay" correctly, adding "please let me . . ." to the original words. "Stay" by Maurice Williams. © 1960 Cheerio Corporation. International copyright secured. All rights reserved. Used by permission.

Canada Council   Conseil des Arts
for the Arts   du Canada

Brindle & Glass Publishing acknowledges the support of the Canada Council for the Arts and the Alberta Foundation for the Arts for our publishing program.

Brindle & Glass Publishing
www.brindleandglass.com

Brindle & Glass is committed to protecting the environment and to the responsible use of natural resources. This book is printed on 100% post-consumer recycled and ancient-forest-friendly paper. For more information please visit www.oldgrowthfree.com.

1 2 3 4 5 08 07 06 05

PRINTED AND BOUND IN CANADA

ABOVE *The Abysmal, Water*

BELOW *The Arousing, Thunder*

Difficulty at the Beginning
works supreme success.

Running
1958–1960

SPRING. WATERY lemon sunlight in the afternoon, throwing a false warmth that's gone by twilight. Clouds unrolling in high sinister patterns, casting a strange greenish light as I sit in study hall tense and filled with foreboding. Then cold driving rain for days at a time and something hurting in me like a spiritual toothache. In the mornings I wake with despair. The days are asking something of me, but I don't know what it is or how to reply. I'm sixteen years old, and I feel caught in a fine mesh net. A tremendous power is flowing underneath me, but I don't know how to touch it. Lyle sniffs the air like a dog, grins at me with wry satisfaction. "Track season," he announces, as though that statement justifies everything, as though our lives have rolled down to that one meaning: to run.

Track season had begun for Lyle during Christmas vacation. He'd run, bogged down and panting, through calf-deep snow up the steep hills behind his house. His method of training was simple: he ran himself into exhaustion. When the weather broke and the snow began to melt, he hitchhiked each Saturday and Sunday to our school to run alone on the sodden track. But now that the track season has opened officially, he has me—his flabby, untrained, and apprehensive protégé—to introduce to the rites of his personal religion.

It's the first day of practice. It might as well be January, drizzling with malignant insistence, half rain, half snow, the

1

temperature in the forties. The coach issues us uniforms, makes a speech about the season, and tells us to go home. That's not for Lyle. "Let's go," he says.

"What?"

"Let's go. You aren't going to let the weather bother you, are you?"

I feel like a fool as I dress, pull on jock and sweat suit, lace up the tennis shoes. Lyle is bounding up and down, swinging his arms. "What a godawful day," he says gleefully. We trot from the gym to the track. I feel as though someone has turned me out in the middle of winter in my underwear. Following Lyle's example, I've wrapped a towel around my neck and ears. "Let's warm up," he says at the track.

We begin jogging on the wet cinders. Above us a sky like dirty whipped cream is on its way somewhere else, moving fast. Soon the snow has misted my glasses so I can barely see Lyle in front of me. He's muttering to himself, turns to make sure I'm behind, calls back, "You jog a lap and then walk a lap until you've finished ten. I'll do a couple slow miles."

We jog one lap together. I stop, and he trots on. I'm panting, discovering to my amazement that I'm warm enough. He laps me as I walk, calls out, "What's the matter?"

"I'm tired."

"Tired," he snorts as though he isn't sure of the meaning of the word, and he's gone down the track.

After five or six laps, even though I'm walking every other one, I'm getting sick at my stomach and dizzy, feeling

2

alternately chilled and feverish. There's a pain in my side like an ice pick. I'm scuttling along like a crab, clutching at my chest. Lyle's finished his two miles, yells at me, "Run it out. Take the pain and run it out. Don't let your form go to hell." He gives me a sample of how I should look: feet pointed straight ahead, long clean strides, hands carried up and reaching as though winding string into the body. "When it hurts, stretch it out."

I finish my last lap. My side is on fire. My lunch is attempting to come up. Lyle supports me with one arm and pushes me along in a fast walk through the wet snow. "Jesus, it hurts," I say.

"Of course it hurts. That's the point. Keep at it. You'll be great. Look at your chest. Good lung capacity. You've got the desire. You'll be really great."

I'm keeping my thoughts to myself. I don't give a damn whether I'll be great or not. What I'd been doing out there— although at the moment it doesn't any longer make the least bit of sense—had been trying to make myself into a real boy, but now I just want the pain to stop and I never want to feel this bad again.

"A year ago," I say, panting, "if somebody had told me . . . that I'd be out for track . . . I'd have laughed in his face."

Lyle gives me a playful push and a sly smile. "You'll be an athlete yet. You've got the spirit." I only groan.

Back at the gym, naked in the showers, he yells to me, "*Mens sana in corpore sano,* right?"

The evening has turned colder when we begin to hitch-hike into town; the air feels as brittle as if we'd stepped back a month into winter, but I'm beginning to enjoy my tiredness. My feet ache with each step; my legs ache all the way up to my hip joints. By the time I get home, all my used muscles will be shaking with light fluttery spasms.

"This is what the church fathers talked about," Lyle is saying. "We don't have a desert, but we have a track."

"I don't know," I say. "Were they after the same thing?"

"Of course they were. *Labore est orare.* It's the only way we have to get at what they were after . . . or the hills." He sweeps one arm up to the distant snow-covered skyline just edged with twilight. "I climb the hills back of my house. I need to be alone to think . . . to pray. It's all got to come from here." He pats his uniformed chest in the vicinity of his heart. "Even running. Concentration. Prayer. It's all the same thing. They tried to tell me that I couldn't play sports by concentration, but they were wrong. That's how I learned everything I know. But you've got to *do it* too. That's been your trouble." He pats his forehead. "All here, nothing in the lungs and legs. But you've got a good heart."

"I don't think I'll ever be that good. I started too late."

"No, no. You've got the spirit. That's the important thing. If you've got that, everything else will follow."

"The spirit's willing, but the flesh is weak," I say, smiling, meaning it as a joke.

"That's what all this is for," he answers in complete seriousness, "to make the flesh match the spirit." Up and down

4

the National Road we can see the snow in the air shaking out like bright splinters.

That was Lyle and I, the beginning of our friendship, track season, our sophomore year. After all these years I still remember that night clearly. By the time I was walking through downtown Raysburg, the ache of my body had turned to joy; tired as I was, I could have run again, laughing, through the streets. I remember crossing the Suspension Bridge over the dark river where the city lights were caught and repeated, the weight of my book bag in my hands, my uniform collar turned up around my ears, the sound of snow crunching under my feet, the sound of automobile tires on the pavement, the tremor of my loosening muscles, my glasses steaming in the moist air of the kitchen when I came in from the cold just in time for dinner.

LYLE AND I had become friends that past winter while hitchhiking into town from school. We both favored a particular spot on the National Road where a traffic light stopped the cars, and we both arrived there after most of the other guys had gone home—he kept late by wrestling practice, I by meetings of the Classical Club or the school newspaper staff. For a few weeks we'd hardly spoken, had simply smiled, nodded, and, by an unstated mutual agreement, hitch-hiked together. Finally one evening, even though we'd been classmates for over a year, he introduced himself formally: "My name's Lyle Ledzinski," holding out a long, bony hand.

I took it. "John Dupre."

"I know," he said, "the brains of the class," and giggled—a sound like a hiccup.

If he knew my reputation, I certainly knew his too. We'd both entered the Academy as freshmen on scholarships with a certain renown preceding us. I was the whiz kid, the straight-A student who'd won every academic prize offered at Jefferson Grade School—"Einstein Junior," as I'd been labeled, a nickname I hated but couldn't shake (although it was a vast improvement over what I'd been called at Jefferson—"*Miss Dupre*"). I'd established myself on the honor roll and had stayed there, firmly entrenched, with not much effort. And Lyle was one of the Polish kids from South Raysburg who made up the core of our football, basketball, and track teams—those tough crazy athletes with unpronounceable last names who formed a nearly exclusive club in the Academy and had weekend adventures that sounded (at least to the ears of a sheltered middle-class bookworm like myself) positively legendary: drunken parties, street fights, stolen beer and stolen hubcaps, encounters with cops. But even in that colorful crowd, Lyle stood out; he'd received the only track scholarship ever given in the history of the school. At fourteen, alone, on a hot summer's day, timed by the coach, watched by his father and our head master, Colonel Sloan, Lyle had run, with no one to pace him, no one to compete against but himself, a five-minute mile.

Lyle was strangely arresting. The most immediate impact of him came from searching eyes that glittered from behind thick glasses; he peered out at the world down a long nose like a night-roaming animal caught by mistake in the daylight. That startled badger effect was accentuated by the adolescent acne that flushed his face. He wasn't especially tall but gave the impression of much greater height because he was thin to the point of emaciation. Later, as I'd get to know him, I'd see how he carried himself—tall and cocky, his head high and back, his great nose sticking up into the air—the stance of the self-proclaimed hero. By emaciation, I don't mean a fragility; he was all knots and knobs, bony joints, hard cords of muscle twisting around his arms like the gnarls of an old tree trunk. He could not possibly have been called handsome, but there was something appealing about him; he was electric and disquieting. He talked with his hands, making frantic passes in the air, his voice high-pitched and strained as though he might break down at any moment. And yet there was, superimposed over all of that tension, such a courtliness and graciousness that I imagined him as an old-world Polish aristocrat.

And he loved to talk. We were interested in the same things. *Life*, we would have said—*Truth*. He'd quote Saint Augustine or Saint Francis; I'd come back with Nietzsche or Freud. We were fascinated with each other. Soon we were more interested in talking than getting home; we'd stop for a Coke in town or just sit by the side of the road without bothering to stick out our thumbs. He kept telling me to go out for track in the spring. Why, I wanted to know. "Because then you'll understand what life's all about." What should I go out for? "The mile," he said as though nothing else was worth considering.

So I went out for track. And kept at it, though God knows why. Eventually I could finish an entire mile without stopping to walk; it took me about ten minutes.

"Don't worry," Lyle said, "it'll come," and then, later in the spring, he invited me to meet him in a bar—which is what I'd wanted all along.

The drinking age in West Virginia was eighteen, but Raysburg in those days was a wide-open town, and there was always a bar somewhere that would serve anyone who walked through the door. The Cat's Eye was at the foot of a narrow flight of stairs in the back of an alley off Short Market Street. I must have paced up and down for an hour, working up my courage to go in. I could hear the distant sound of rock 'n roll. Kids passed me on their way in or out, but no one I knew. Sometimes I had trouble convincing people that I was even *sixteen*, and I kept wondering what I'd say if somebody asked to see my draft card. I was literally shaking with fear, but I knew I had to do it. Walking back that alley and down those stairs took nearly everything I had.

The bar was loud, that was the first impression: thunderous jukebox, yelling high-school kids. After a moment I located Lyle. He was sitting at a corner table, waving a beer bottle at me. I threaded my way through the crowd, mostly boys but some girls too, more than I'd expected—high heels, tight skirts, lots of makeup. A wild set, I thought, thrilled. And everybody in the whole damned place looked older than I did. "Can we really get served?" I asked, amazed.

"Just have to be tall enough to reach the bar," Lyle said.

He ordered four more beers. "My, my, my," he said, smacked his lips and rubbed his long hands together. We each drank one quickly, hardly stopping to breathe. "Do you feel anything?"

"Not a thing," I said and drank the beer desperately, waiting for some kind of effect. I suspected that the times before when I'd tried to convince myself I'd been drunk, nipping at my father's bourbon in the middle of the night, I hadn't been drunk at all, at least not on the alcohol. This time I wanted to experience it fully, have no doubt in my mind that I'd done it. We ordered another round. I didn't much like the taste of the stuff.

I was counting carefully. I drank five beers in less than fifteen minutes. "You're going to get smashed out on your ass," Lyle said. That sounded like a very funny thing to say; I began to giggle. Halfway through the sixth beer, I found suddenly that the world was profoundly altered. I laughed outright, fell back in my chair. Here it was. For the first time in my life I was drunk—unbelievably, gloriously drunk. "Cut it out," Lyle said. "People will think you're drunk."

That was the funniest thing I'd ever heard in my life. "This is great," I managed to shout between spasms of laughter.

Lyle was getting alarmed. "Let's get out of here," he hissed. I made an effort to put on a poker face, and he hustled me upstairs and outside.

The open air, rather than sobering me, made me drunker. I walked into the indigo night waving my arms and yelling;

the exhilaration was so great I could find no way to express it except by screaming with laughter. The world was filled with a savage power; I'd sensed it before but had never felt it that clearly. We walked quickly into East Raysburg, and I loved everything I saw. Those wretched narrow gutters of streets, the full garbage cans, the decrepit houses, the polluted sky above them, the light itself—contrast between the blue-black overcast and the yellow of windows—the phone poles and power lines: it was all beautiful. No, not beautiful—ugly, awful, disgusting, and I loved it. If this was *life,* this world as it looked then, the state I was in, then I wanted more of it. I would have jumped into a sewer to get it.

Eventually I got control of myself. "Let's go back," I said. "Are you all right?"

"Sure, I'm all right." We turned around and ran back to the Cat's Eye—back the alleys, down the stairs, and through the jam of yelling underaged kids to wedge ourselves around a table in the corner. The jukebox, kicking out that wonderful rock 'n roll, was perfect for the way I was feeling.

We ordered enough beer to cover the table top. Lyle was getting drunk too. His eyes were glittering; sweat was pouring down his face; he was shaking with excitement. We spotted a beautiful hoodlum girl standing with her friends across the room. She was dark, could have been Italian, and was wearing a skirt so tight I couldn't imagine how she'd squeezed herself into it. "Look at that," I said.

"My, my, my," Lyle said. We stared at her, fascinated. She reminded me, once again, of how much I wanted to have a girlfriend, some Chantilly-lace, pretty-face sweetheart like the one the Big Bopper sang about, Chuck Berry's sweet sixteen sporting bright red lipstick and high heels, or a majorette who'd walk into the Friday Night Hop after the football game still wearing her uniform, her legs, under her deliciously short skirt, pink with cold, those wonderful tasseled white boots on her feet. Or, if I couldn't have one of those wet-dream lovelies, any ordinary girl would do, any of the Canden or Raysburg High kids I saw on the bus with their pony tails and bobby socks. Drunk as I was, the full force of my desire struck me: *I want a girl.* I had an image of myself exploding from sheer frustration to leap, screaming, into the Ohio River.

Lyle must have been thinking something similar. "You go out with anybody?" he said.

"No. Do you?"

"Yeah. Sort of." He shrugged dismissively, toasted me with his beer bottle. "May this be the year of piece." It took me a minute to get the joke.

We stayed until the bar closed, yelling short bursts of words at each other over the noise. I was forcing myself to drink as much as I could as fast as I could, and the more I drank, the more I felt that anything was possible. Running track was possible. Being a real boy was possible. Having a girlfriend was possible. I was feeling for the first time the total movement of drunkenness (which later was to become hauntingly familiar), beginning to know the bits of physical sensation that blend to make this movement: the bitter tang of the beer, the music like a visible force hammering in the room, the smoke burning and blurring the eyes, the shouting voice of the bar, the charge of electricity in the air— beginning to know the mental expansions, breaking of constraint, the sudden possibilities of thought, events interconnecting in a peculiar and supra-lucid pattern. And I felt for the first time the power of our talk—these shouted statements—taking off like a roller coaster on the force of this movement, expanding out and twisting into new and unexpected directions. I've never found the words for the moment of realization (from nowhere, with no warning) that we've become bathed in a numinous power, a devastating glory, that I've lived all of my life to arrive at this instant, this passing breath of time, that this NOW completely justifies—more than that, glorifies—everything.

Lyle was yelling at me across the table, words that look trivial when put down on paper, but at the time full of power and truth: "We've got to know . . . all of *life!*"

Walking home afterward, across the bridge, I felt shattered. I had never suspected that it could be like this.

June, 1958

MY HAIR'S too short. I've worked a healthy handful of brilliantine through it, brushed it, combed it, and it's not too bad on top, but there's nothing I can do about the back and sides except wait. By the time I've grown a good thick DA, it'll be fall and I'll have to cut it off for school. The disadvantages of the Academy, I'm thinking, are beginning to outweigh the advantages. My father had sent me out there to make me manly, and, to both his surprise and mine, I'd eventually grown to like the place—but now I'm no longer a child who finds the uniforms and toy guns exciting, and I've begun to hate it more than ever when I run into Raysburg High kids on the street and they chant after me that ancient rhyme going all the way back (so he'd told me) to my father's day:

> Hup, two, three! Hup, two, three!
> We're the boys from the Academy.
> We don't smoke, and we don't chew.
> And we don't go with girls that do.

So maybe Raysburg High doesn't have the most elevated academic standards in the Valley, but at least the guys who go there aren't required to keep their hair cut down to military length. But most significantly—they go to school every day with girls.

There's an apologetic tap on the bathroom door. "Oh, Christ," I say silently, forming the words for myself in the mirror. Out loud: "Yeah."

My mother opens the door six inches. "You aren't going to be really late again tonight are you, honey?"

"No."

I wait until she shuts the door. Then I roll up the short sleeves of my pink shirt one turn, fold up the collar high behind my neck, unbutton another button to show more of the hair that's begun to appear on my chest. Watching myself in the full-length mirror, I push my jeans lower on my hips. Half-inch black belt buckled on the left side, polished engineer boots on my feet, I slouch against the wall, studying the effect, trying for that perfect mask of sullen boredom and hostility: James Dean. I hear my mother in the living room playing the piano. It's Debussy, one of those pieces she plays interminably, always getting stuck in the same place, always blowing the same run, always starting over. The sound of that piano can drive me frantic.

On the way to my bedroom, I hear my father yell, "Hey, Elvis."

I decide to be amused. "Yeah, Dad?"

"Another big night?"

"Never can tell."

My mother blows the run again and starts over. Her back's to us; we could be in another world. My father's sitting on the couch, his feet up on the coffee table, the paper in his lap. Within easy reach of his right hand is the coffee cup left over from dinner; it's there every night. By now it has more Jim Beam in it than coffee, but neither I nor my mother is supposed to notice. He looks up at me grinning: pink round face, chocolate-brown Dupre eyes, hair perfectly parted. "Need a buck?" he says.

"Wouldn't hurt."

He digs a five out of his wallet, folds it with a snap, and pushes it at me. It's a brand-new bill, fresh and crisp as if it's just come off the press. I can never get over how perfectly he keeps his nails. He wears an amethyst ring on his left hand, smells of hair tonic, Old Spice, and whiskey. He sends me a broad wink. "Watch yourself."

"Sure." In a hour or so my mother will go to bed with a Reader's Digest Condensed Novel. My father will lay aside the paper and, whistling some old tune between his teeth— "Yes sir, that's my baby!"—will smooth back his hair with his set of matching brushes, knot up his tie, put on his suit jacket, and slip out of the house. Then he and I will be doing the same thing: getting drunk. We'll never run into each other though, because I'll either be sitting in the dark corner of a Polish bar or walking the alleys of South Raysburg and he'll be on the other side of a locked door with a one-way mirror—in the Twenty-one, playing poker. Sunday morning we'll face each other across the breakfast table with unspoken hangovers. I'll be able to tell right away whether he won or lost.

Out front the horn's already blowing.

"Hey, why doesn't that kid ever come up here?" my father says sourly. He's afraid he's not good enough for the son of the Revingtons. He's right, and I'm already down the stairs.

"What say, old man?"

"Evening, William."

"Check the back."

I look. Four quarts. Revington knows the bartender in the Oval. "A good night, William, a good night. Are we going to get drunk, or what?"

"We're not merely going to get drunk, we're going to get juiced out on our asses. I came in last night and the old man said, 'Tell me, William, what are you doing drunk on Friday night?' I said, 'Well, Dad, it's like this. I'm just getting started early for Saturday.'"

Revington's the class wise-ass. He'd been my only friend when I'd first showed up at the Academy, and he's still my friend—although sometimes I wonder why. I'm certainly not the colorful character he is. At sixteen, he's already six feet tall; in a school that demands a ramrod-stiff posture, he slouches down the halls like a twenties lounge lizard. His jet-black hair is always too long, always falling in his face. He has a way of looking at our teachers—simply looking at them with an amused, superior glint in his dark eyes and the faintest suggestion of a smile on his lips—that drives them absolutely nuts. Most afternoons he can be found on the road in front of the Old Main, marching off an hour of punishment duty.

Out of town, up High Light Road to drink the first quart, we're singing along with the car radio. Revington, hunched over the wheel playing fighter pilot, screams us around that insanely curving West Virginia road—sheer rock face on one side, forty foot drop-off on the other. He talks to me out of the side of his mouth in one of his movie voices. "*Girls,* old man . . . Canden High girls . . . the whole frigging lot of them."

"Yeah, but I wasn't invited."

"Invited?" he says, laughing. "Who says *I* was invited?

16

She has to let me in. *Her* family knows *my* family." It's the out-the-pike crowd he's talking about, the rich kids; he's one of them himself. His father's a big shit at Raysburg Steel; one uncle's a lawyer, one's a doctor, and one owns a bank. He's the only guy I know who lives on a street with his own name on it: Revington Crescent. "You said you wanted to meet girls, Dupre . . ." He shrugs.

"Let's see who's at the Inn first," hedging because I'd told Lyle I'd meet him.

Two quarts gone, we park on Short Market Street. High school kids—all male—lounge about on the sidewalk grouped by school: Canden on that corner, Raysburg High on this one, the boys from the Academy leaning against the wall under the Capitol Theater marquee. Every ten minutes or so the prowl car slides by easy as silk. The girls have to walk the gauntlet, past all those hungry eyes and up the stairs to Gerry's Inn.

"What do you say, gentlemen? Any action?"

"Shit. Nothing."

"Been out yet?" Meaning: for a drink.

"Not yet. Later. Hey, you drunk again, Dupre?"

"Who me? Goddamned filthy rumor."

Lyle's drawing me aside to say in an excited whisper, "Hey, boy, what are you doing with *him?*" He doesn't like Revington. "We're going down to South Raysburg later. Kruszka's uncle works in a hole down there. He'll slip us something out the back. What do you say?"

"Shit, he wants me to go to a party with him."

Lyle looks down his big nose at me, disapproving. It's not just money and family, it's that Revington can never take anything seriously, particularly can't take athletics seriously. He's our only pole-vaulter of any note, but he doesn't care, doesn't train, and for Lyle that's something that can't be understood or forgiven.

"*Canden High* girls," Lyle says in a hissing, disgusted voice. He doesn't approve of them either.

It costs a lot to go to the Academy; most of the students come from families with money, but the school does give scholarships, athletic ones to tough Polish boys from South Raysburg, academic ones to straight-A students like our few token Jewish kids—and me. It makes for an uneasy mix. I'm one of the few guys who can move from group to group, but not without a certain friction. "You're going to blow it loafing with him," Lyle says.

It makes me angry. "Damn it, boy, I've got to meet some women." Christ, where does Lyle get off with this shit? He has a steady girl, doesn't he? Shirley Pulenski—a slight blond kid with blue-framed glasses. Lyle, who seems to adore her with a passion only slightly less exalted than a monk might feel for the Virgin Mary, had told me (embarrassed, giggling in that high-pitched strained way of his) that before asking her to the Christmas dance he had prostrated himself in front of the picture of Jesus in his bedroom and prayed that he would be worthy.

Back in Revington's car up Raysburg Hill, over the speed limit, running the red light at the top. I'm feeling like a traitor, my loyalties torn. "Where are we going? Who's having this party?" I've figured out that I'm being used as a pawn in one of Revington's practical jokes; he's planned the whole thing—going to turn up with some hoodlum friend reeking of beer, walk in and show off his cool. I'm dressed like a hood, so I'll do, but *anybody* would do. Shit, I should have stayed with Lyle.

"Don't sweat it, Dupre." He locks it up and screams into the curb, grins at me, pushes back his hair, lights a cigarette. "Kicks," he says. Fuck you, I think. My mouth's gone dry. It's a long way from my parents' place on Raysburg Island to this neighborhood. He hands me the quart and I kill it.

A girl meets us at the door, obviously the young lady of the house, a ponytail blond in heels and a cocktail dress. She's probably our age. "Good evening, Barbara," Revington says in an affected drawling voice. He's posed himself, the entire skinny length of him, leaning against the doorjamb. He trails a languid hand with cigarette in it, pointing at me. "My friend, Johnny Dupre. Mind if we come in?" The girl steps back from the door; her face has fallen completely apart. Revington smiles down at her like a British actor. It's the first time I've understood exactly who he is—his effortless good looks, his boneless elegance, the way he wears his clothes, no matter how casual, as though he's Fred Astaire in a tuxedo; it's what my mother calls "breeding."

"William," the girl says, her eyes blinking rapidly. One hand, painted nails, is stopped halfway to her face. He knows that she knows that she has to let him in, and it *is* funny, damn it, but I won't be able to laugh until later.

She pushes a smile back on, and we follow her down to the rec room. The parents are discreetly nowhere to be seen. We walk through the door, the party freezes over, but the record player keeps going, slaps down another forty-five. Nobody's dancing, everybody's looking at us, and Revington's in his element, so pleased with himself that he can't keep the laughter out of his voice. With a light touch on my elbow, he guides me forward. He seems to know all the girls. "Good evening, Sue. You look ravishing tonight . . . Good evening, Janice. Good evening, Robin." For the boys, he hasn't got a word.

All right, so if I have to play, I'll play. I lean against the wall next to the chip-dip and Cokes, slowly unwind myself as though there's infinite time, as though all of this is beneath me, as though I might be so drunk that I could use some help from the wall for a moment—but only for a moment. The new kid in town, the outsider, Jimmy himself. I yawn, cross my legs, slouch just as I've practiced in the mirror. Then, with great deliberateness, with what I hope's just the faintest suggestion of menace, I look around the room. Yeah, I'm out of place; every guy there is wearing a sports jacket and tie; a couple of them are big, look like they play center for Canden; they're eying me with a menace that's more than suggestion. The girls are in summer dresses or jumpers with frilly blouses, set hair or ponytails, makeup, nylons and heels. They're immaculate.

Gradual thaw, the dancing begins again, and Revington's

hustling the girl of the house, the one named Barbara; he's got her uncomfortably backed into a corner. I'm being ignored, carefully and pointedly. It's no joke: I *am* drunk, but nowhere near drunk enough. I don't know how long I can continue to stand there posed against the wall. I yawn again; inside I'm cold and contracted, thinking: Goddamn you, William Revington. But then I begin to see sideways glances from the girls; they're checking me out, so quick and subtle I can't quite catch them at it—brushing of bee wings.

A little girl on the far side of the room is sitting on the couch with her knees together, her feet pointed, her long legs arranged as perfectly as if she's posing for a picture. My first thought: How did *she* get in here? Must be somebody's kid sister. Her turquoise blue dress is like a child's party frock— too many petticoats—and the skirt's above her knees. It's the shortest skirt in the room. On her feet, ballerinas the color of her dress and flat as paper. She meets my eyes and doesn't look away. I can't look away either. She has the most beautiful eyes I've ever seen, enormous and shining. In a single stiffly explosive movement she jumps to her feet and walks directly toward me, rustling as she comes.

She's not wearing either socks or nylons—oddly bare-legged—and those huge eyes turn out to be as blue as her dress. Her straight taffy-colored hair hasn't been curled; it's cut off into ruler-straight bangs that cover her eyebrows, cut off at her shoulders—an abrupt unflattering pageboy, a little kid's haircut, makes her narrow face seem even narrower, accentuates the long straight nose. Pale skin, nearly white, faint spray of freckles, but cheeks flushed with excitement. She's painted her lips a screaming Marilyn-Monroe scarlet, lipstick laid on without compromise, and no other makeup to soften it—just those tense lips frozen into a smile like shiny red enamel slathered onto a marble statue. She can't possibly be older than twelve. "Hi," she says, "do you want to dance?"

Now what the hell can I do with that? The other girls are giving each other knowing grins, and I can feel the social lines crisscrossing the room like a spider web—whispering voices, oblique glances. Up close, her face is a mask of strain: flaring nostrils, haze of sweat on her upper lip. *You're a loser, kid,* I think, and to gain time slowly push myself away from the wall.

I know if I dance with her, I'll lose everything too—my image, my cool, the works—and that Revington won't protect me. If I dance with this girl, I'll join at once in her ignominious status; instead of the tough aloof stranger, I'll be a jerk, a clown. The other girls are staring openly now, whispering and giggling, waiting with a breathless eagerness I can feel in the air for me to give her the brush-off. Even some of the boys are beginning to look. Suddenly I know how much I hate all of them. "Sure," I say to her.

Her relief is so obvious that it hurts me to see it. It's a slow dance; I take her into my arms and smell the sharp tangy perfume, much too much of it, and underneath, the stink of her fear. Her voice is bouncy and bright. "I really like this song, don't you? I'm really glad you said you'd dance with me right away before it ended." She presses in tight to me, finds my crotch at once, wiggles into it with one of her long legs. I'm so astonished that it takes me most of the song to get an erection. I let my right hand drift down her side. A tiny waist. And that flare to her hips is not a twelve-year-old's. Her voice is moist and warm in my ear: "My name's Linda Edmonds, what's yours?"

A WEEK later, the voice over the phone was so loud and frightened that it took me a long time to recognize it, connect it with the image of the young girl I'd met. "I didn't think you were going to call me," she said.

I almost hadn't called her. "Jesus Christ, John," Revington had said to me after we'd left, "what the hell were you doing *with Linda Edmonds?*"

"I thought you'd think it was funny, William."

"But do you know how old she is, for fuck's sake? She's just out of the eighth grade."

I was saved by the magic of numbers, found out that she'd turned fourteen less than a month before I met her—which put her barely over the line. (By some unwritten law, fourteen was considered the absolute downward limit by the guys in my class.) But she was nothing to brag about. Except for the overdone lipstick, she'd been dressed like a child, and, to put it kindly, she didn't have much of a figure. She did have a pretty face, but only that—pretty. So what if her eyes were fantastic, her legs long and lovely, and her dancing excruciatingly provocative? I certainly couldn't walk into Gerry's Inn with her, introduce her to Lyle, or take her to the prom. I couldn't imagine taking her anywhere. So what was it about her that kept me from falling asleep at night, that made me call her up every day or two?

From those brief tense conversations in which I had to do most of the work because she seemed scarcely able to speak at all, I collected only a few trivial facts: that she was an only child, that she had a dog named Lady and a cat named Sooty, that she took ballet lessons five days a week, that she'd been the first girl in her class to go on pointe. I'd sit with my eyes shut listening to her strained voice, her breathless dangling sentences, and try to remember exactly what she'd looked like walking toward me with the rustle of all those petticoats, exactly what it had felt like to have her leg pressed tight into my crotch. Both an awkward little kid and the most forward girl I'd ever met, but that formulation didn't explain a damned thing. I couldn't understand why I couldn't stop thinking about her.

Finally, after a million phone calls, I said, "Hey, Linda . . . can I see you again?" There was a pause on the line so long that I began to wonder if she'd laid down the phone and walked away. Then she said, "I think you'd better meet my parents."

I knew enough to put on a suit and tie. I drove my father's clunker Dodge into a neighborhood where I'd never been, into a huge circular street with a park in the middle and houses that looked as though the antebellum half of *Gone With the Wind* could have been shot there. I pulled up and checked the address, and by God that was it. The affluent home where I'd met her dwindled into nothingness, became as insignificant as a peasant cottage; her front lawn looked as big as a golf course. I parked, walked up the flagstone path, up the concrete steps, up the white wooden steps, passed between the Doric columns, and confronted the brass door knocker with "Edmonds" engraved on it.

I had asked my father, "Hey, do you know a Charles Edmonds?"

"Do you mean Charlie Edmonds?"

"I don't know. Maybe that's who I mean."

"Well, if that's who you mean, he's one of the vice presidents of Raysburg Steel."

I honest to God expected a butler to open the door, but there was Linda herself. It was a shock to see her again. I realized that I'd gone over the night I'd met her so much that it had taken on a polished legendary quality, and the process had distanced her. Now, suddenly, I saw those enormous blue eyes, those geometrically straight bangs, that thin pale faintly canine face, all of it confirming what I remembered, but no memory of her could be as profound and mysteriously human as her immediate presence in front of me. This was serious. She was wearing a plain white blouse, a pleated tartan skirt, knee socks and loafers—no lipstick this time: a little kid, flat as a board, her hands shaking. She couldn't even smile. "Hi," she said miserably, "come in."

When I'd been admitted to the Academy, I'd had an interview with Colonel Sloan: six feet four, silver-white hair, back stiff as a Confederate rifle, orotund preacher's voice. He'd scared the shit out of me, continued to scare the shit out of me all through high school, and if I met him today the way he was then—even though I know better—he'd still scare the shit out of me. That interview in the Colonel's office remains in memory as one of the worst moments of my life. The interview with Linda's parents was worse. The living room had wall-to-wall carpeting, a collection of antique glass, and a full-sized grand piano. The picture window wasn't quite as big as a movie screen. I couldn't imagine how anybody in their right mind could call Linda's father "Charlie." Her mother was wearing a suit complete with the jacket; her straight skirt was very tight, her spike heels very high, her long red nails as perfect as if they'd been painted an hour ago. I'd never seen anything like her outside the pages of a fashion magazine. I was doing my best to be the perfect Academy cadet, *sir* and *ma'am* and winning smile and looking them in the eye. Linda's mother kept saying things like: "Dupre? . . . Do I know your family?"

It was beginning to make me mad, and I heard myself saying: "We've lived in West Virginia five generations." I think she heard what I didn't say: How long have *you* lived here? Mrs. Edmonds had a reputation as a stunningly beautiful woman; I could understand why, but I never found her beautiful. Her eyes narrowed noticeably, and she gave me the look a royal equestrienne might give a horse that's just kicked at her.

Underneath my smile I was furious, thinking: Yeah, I'll bet you *do* know my family. Maybe you've bought a used car or some Alcoa aluminum siding from my father or run into

26

him at two in the morning in the back room of somebody's bar; or maybe you know about my grandfather, the professional gambler who vanished in his seventies, only to be found, a few years later, in a rented room in Lexington, Kentucky, surrounded by Baptist bible tracts and three weeks dead of cirrhosis of the liver; or maybe you've heard of my great-grandfather, the first John Dupre, who was said to have killed a man in a gun fight? I was strangely proud of my seedy family with its drunken sweet-talking uncles, batty fading aunts, and a thousand fractious cousins. So I thought: Who the hell are *you*, Mrs. Charles Edmonds, to come into my home town from the state of New York and ask me who my family is?

I never called her father anything but "Mr. Edmonds," and I think he came to like me in his distant way. Raysburg Steel ate him up, and he wasn't around much. We played chess one night—only once. He opened with his king's knight's pawn, and I knew I had him. I fianchettoed both bishops and chopped up his center with them. He allowed two passed pawns, and I rammed them down his throat, exchanged him down to nothing, and mated him in half an hour. It changed something, and he respected me after that. But Mrs. Edmonds and I knew each other from that very first night, and nothing ever changed. We were always enormously polite to each other, even to the very end. We couldn't have hated each other more if we'd been the last contending survivors of a twelve-generation clan war.

They finally left us alone. It had been hard on Linda too;

I didn't think she was going to be able to say anything.

"So you're going to be a freshman, huh?" I said.

She pulled herself together—I could see her doing it—and, as suddenly as if I'd pushed a GO button, out came the bright rapid chatter. "Oh, I'm so glad I'm going to be in high school. I'm really looking forward to it. You're going to be a junior, aren't you? I'm kind of scared. Everybody says it's so different, they expect so much more of you. Do you think that's true? Canden's such a big school. I wonder if I'll get lost out there."

I tried to imagine what it must be like for her—leaving safe little Meadowland Grade School—tried to remember how I'd felt when I'd first gone to the Academy. And then the full force of it struck me. When I'd been *her age*, I'd been a dreamy little kid with no friends, my entire life focused inward, a science fiction reader, confused and miserable, still desperately wanting to be a girl. *My* first year in high school had been sheer hell.

She walked skitterishly around the living room, doing God knows what, picking up a magazine and putting it down somewhere else, straightening a doily. She offered me hard candy in a blue dish. I didn't eat candy but took a piece anyway. And she quickly turned down a framed photograph on the piano so I couldn't see it, then sat down immediately with me on the couch again, close. I took her hand. She let me.

"Why'd you keep calling me?" she said. "Why did you want to see me?"

I hadn't expected her to be that direct, and I didn't know

the answers to those questions. "I think you're beautiful," was all I could find, a line like something my father would have used.

"Who, me? Maybe you'd better have your glasses checked." But I could tell that she was pleased. After a moment: "I'm too young for you."

"Who says? Your mother?" She didn't answer. "Why'd you come over to dance with me?"

"I thought you were cute."

Now *I* was pleased. "Do you still think so?"

In the tone of "What a dumb question": "Of course."

"Can I see you again?"

She had a hard time with that. When she answered, it was as though she'd decided on the truth, having run through a number of alternatives. "I'll see you . . . as much as my mother will let me."

The picture she'd turned down stayed in my mind; weeks later I'd get to see it—a tinted portrait of her with a ribbon in her Shirley Temple curls, short white gloves, a petticoated dress a foot above her knees, anklets and black patent shoes, posed on a chair. It took her a year to tell me that it hadn't been taken when she'd been ten, as I'd thought, but when she'd been twelve, just as it took her a year to tell me that the reason she'd been barelegged the night I'd met her had been because she'd taken off the white socks her mother had made her wear and stuffed them into her purse. I found out about the lipstick right away though because she kept it in the glove compartment of my car—I mean my father's car. He found it, of course, and kidded me endlessly: "Are you sure it's the right color for you, John?"

You didn't kiss nice girls on first dates; everybody knew that, so I wasn't even thinking of it that night at her house, but she kissed me. She stepped outside and closed the front door—not tight, not enough to make a noise, just enough to be sure that we couldn't be seen—and without any preliminaries, grabbed me. I bent to give her a brotherly peck and met her open mouth, her tongue on mine. She fled back inside and left me standing, blazing away like a distress flare, on that broad white porch.

LYLE AND I gradually began to have a profound, even shattering, influence on each other. He convinced me that to find what we were after, a physical and bodily search was as important as a mental one. He disturbed me with his strange Catholic mysticism, inspired me with such intense faith that I suspended my inherent skepticism dozens of times. Once, at the height of a blistering summer heat wave, he insisted that we fast all day, then walk to the Academy and run until we couldn't run any more—and eat toothpaste in between laps. I thought he was totally out of his mind. I did it. In fact, if he'd appeared one day for morning formation wearing a loincloth and had invited me to accompany him into the wilderness, I might very well have done that too. And I widened his narrow parochial school background, could catch the flaws in his arguments, refer to writers he'd never heard of. As half-baked as I was then, I must have appeared profoundly learned to him. I gave him new ideas. He took them, tore them apart, and gave them back to me—on fire.

We were chameleons, changing roles faster than understudies for the *commedia dell'arte*. I vacillated between a tough guy pose, which couldn't have been further from the truth, and that of an urbane man of the world. Lyle was half a dozen people, from Saint John of the Cross to cool investigator (he always had a science project going—studying the effect of acids on seed germination, collecting rocks and fossils, measuring the rainfall) to beer-guzzling hood. Halfway through our third year of Latin, we studded our speech with . Latin phrases like seminary students, his always mangled through the warp of his Polish tongue. (He could never pronounce anything right: Modigliani came out Mo-diddlyani; Kerouac became Kerolic, to rhyme with alcoholic.) We were playing games with a passion, light-hearted on the surface—underneath, deadly serious.

William Revington was my other close friend, and, although I managed to get him and Lyle together a few times, even drunk together, they never liked or trusted each other. I'd grown up so imbued with the myth of a democratic America that it wasn't until I looked back on it, years later, that it occurred to me that the tension between them could have been explained by a phrase as old and flat-footed as "class differences." But I was becoming identified with the Polish contingent; even something of the magic of athletics was beginning to rub off on me. It wasn't required that I be a winner, I discovered, only that I try: "Dupre? Oh yeah, he runs track. The mile." And it didn't hurt the bad-ass reputation I was cultivating that I occasionally drank until I passed out cold.

That fall some fuse that had been smoldering through childhood caught and my junior year took off like a roman candle. The image is Kerouac's, and that was the year we read him. Like James Dean (another of our heroes), Kerouac had the perfect blend of outward toughness, inward sentimentality. We were on his wavelength; he was just as fucked-up as we were, so we swallowed his mythology whole. When we betrayed each other, it was Dean leaving Sal sick in Mexico. When we hit the street for the weekend, we were out for, of course, our kicks. When we were filled with despair, we were dying along with Jack down in Denver. We made a fetish of experience as an end in itself, tried to say a resounding Dean Moriarity "Yes!" to everything.

I felt my horizons expanding like an endless sunrise; I was moving constantly, either mentally or physically, and the biggest part of that movement was talk. At the core of any conversation would be Lyle, Joe Kruszka, and myself with Kupla, Dutkiewicz, Czetwertynski and the others circling around. We talked before school, walking around the track; although we were supposed to maintain a decorous military silence, we talked in the halls between classes; we talked all lunch period in, of all places, the can, leaning against the radiator across from the urinals, and, of course, we talked in the gym locker rooms and afterward, going home. Then later, in the middle of the evening when we were supposed to be doing our homework, we couldn't let it lie, had to get on the phone and keep on going until eleven or twelve at night, only to fall into bed exhausted to snatch a few hours of sleep in order to get ready for the session the next day.

The weekends were frantic; we began to prepare for them on Wednesday. By Friday afternoon we couldn't have concentrated on a classroom discussion if it had been led by the Pope. A hysterical pulse shook the halls; voices came drifting around corners with half sentences which had the import of Cabalistic utterances; demonic laughter filtered from another floor. We were planning the great, unbelievable, marvelous, and indescribably daring times we were going to have, how much we were going to drink, how drunk we were going to get. If, on Monday morning, we were not bleary-eyed, drooping, weary—in short, totally demolished for any activity except another six hours of sleep, we thought we hadn't had a good time over the weekend.

We talked about the mysteries of the Catholic Church (far more mysterious to me than to any of the kids who'd been raised in the faith), Plato's Dialogues (How should we live?), and sex. All of us knew guys who actually fucked, but they were always *somebody else*. At any rate, it was impossible to sort the truth from the lies. "Did you get in her pants? No shit! And then what did she do? Really got your finger in, huh? Don't shit me now, man!"

I don't know what I ran on in those days, sheer nervous energy perhaps. I somehow managed to get the schoolwork done (after a fashion), to read two or three extra books a week, talk to Lyle or Revington or anybody else handy every possible waking moment, get drunk twice over the weekends, lift weights in the gym, go out for track—and still I had time to take Linda out and think about her constantly. If I had a hard time fitting Lyle and Revington together, I had a harder time fitting Linda anywhere. Revington thought she was a bad joke, a pampered little rich kid, an infantile baby doll. And I was afraid to find out what Lyle or any of the Polish contingent would think; they knew I was dating, but I refused to talk about her. Her little-girl chatter, her bright-eyed naivety, all her family's goddamned money— it was impossible. I kept her to myself. But in the night I replayed, in a deliciously detailed anguish, every nuance of those exploratory kisses we stole when we could evade the eyes of her bitch of a mother. Only the rock 'n roll singers on the radio understood what I was feeling. Maurice Williams recorded the perfect song; I bought his record and played the grooves off it. His high-pitched whining voice was the quintessence of a desire that could go on and on without an end in sight—burning. With no hope of release—burning. After all possibility of endurance is gone—burning. "Please let me *stay* . . . just a little bit longer."

I WAS always attracted to extremes, willing to follow any promising line of thought as far as I could, no matter how strange the journey. But Lyle, when I first knew him (strangely enough, for all his insane Catholic fervor), would go only so far and then pull back.

One afternoon at the tail end of winter, a sunny Saturday predicting spring, Lyle borrowed his father's car, picked me up, and we took off for a drive into the country. His father, a worried man, had made Lyle wait until he was seventeen to get his driver's license and then had told him plainly never to take the car out of town. So here we were, the first chance we got, headed out of town.

The car broke down just outside of Barnesville. We found a kid to help us fix it, one of those teenage automotive wizards who can repair anything with a set of open-end wrenches and a big hammer. While the kid was puttering around under the hood, I was playing the cool role, beginning every sentence with "man." Lyle stood by and wrung his hands.

When we started home, Lyle was so furious with me that he couldn't speak, clutched the steering wheel so hard his knuckles turned white, and stared straight ahead at the road. "How could you?" he began finally, "How could you do that? Playing so damned BEAT!"

"You were doing it yourself on the way out."

"That was different. But after the car broke down, HOW COULD YOU?"

"Lyle," I said, beginning as calmly as I could, "what do you think it is, a game?"

"Yes," he shouted, "a game."

"Well, for me it's more than a game. It's a pose, yes, but it's got to be a *real* pose or it doesn't mean a thing. And if it breaks down at the first sign of trouble, it doesn't mean a thing . . . It's just a child's game, and we're just a couple kids playing grown up." I knew by taking that line that I was adding fuel to the fire, but I couldn't resist.

"It's not your father's car," he shouted back at me.

"That's true," I said, "but even if it was, I would've done exactly the same thing, said exactly the same thing."

He said nothing, so I went on. "A couple years ago I kept trying to take certain books out of the library, the forbidden books, you know . . . Nietzsche, Freud . . . and the old bitch wouldn't let me. I talked to her about it, and . . . well, what she seemed to be saying was that at my age I'd probably take Nietzsche seriously, but when I got to her age I'd know better and could read him with a 'mature mind.' I guess that means a mind that can play with ideas without taking them seriously. Do you understand me?" He still didn't say anything, but I could see that I'd hit him.

"If you're looking for *Truth*," I said, pressing my point, "and you find an idea that appears to be true, then you've *got* to put it into practice, try to make it live in your life, or you're the worst kind of hypocrite."

I went on in this vein for a while. Lyle said nothing, stared straight ahead at the road. Finally, he burst out, "I don't care about any of that, but it's not worth fighting about."

"Of course it isn't. But don't you see what I'm saying?"

"I see what you're saying, but let's just forget it."

He drove in silence for a few miles. Then, with his voice shaking: "You just think I'm a dumb Polack, don't you?"

"Jesus Christ, Lyle, how'd you ever . . .?"

"Why don't you want me to meet your girl?"

Now *I* felt like the hypocrite. "Sure," I said slowly, "if you want to."

"I introduced you to Shirley, didn't I?"

"Of course you did. Damn it, I just didn't think it was important."

"You and your *Truth,*" he said. "Are we friends or not? Why don't you put *that* into practice?"

By the time we got back to Raysburg, the storm between us was over. We stopped into the New Moon Cafe for fish sandwiches and beer. Lyle was suddenly buoyant again. "You're right," he kept saying, "we've got to move." Which isn't what I'd been saying at all. But I nodded and agreed with him.

Just before we parted that day, he said, "Damn it, let's not fight. Your friendship's more important than any of this."

"More important than your father's car?" I couldn't help asking.

"Of course," he said in perfect seriousness. "Of course it is. And look, I don't care whether I meet your girlfriend or not."

"You'll meet her. I promise."

He caught my hand and looked at me intently. I was tempted to laugh but didn't. "That's one thing we should never forget," he said. "We've got to stick together."

"Right, Lyle," I said, smiling. I was suddenly ashamed at my impulse to laugh at him.

LYLE LEDZINSKI: "The Mad Polack," we had taken to calling him, and when we wanted to flatter him, "The

Golden Polack." He was one of my best friends, my brother, a person so important in my life that I can't imagine being the way I am today if I hadn't met him. With his passion, his energy, his craziness, he was magnificent, but he could also be a pain in the ass.

Phone call at four in the morning. I stagger up to answer, grab the phone, and there he is on the other end, crying. "This is Lyle."

"I know, for Christ's sake."

"Hey, I'm sorry to call you . . ."

"That's all right. I was sound asleep so don't expect . . ."

"I just had to talk to somebody."

"OK. What the hell's the matter?"

"They threw me out. Out! Out! Out! Out of the house. What am I going to do? Where am I going to go?"

I can hear a truck roll by on his end of the line. "Where are you?"

"Twenty-second Street. I've been walking . . . What can I do? Has there ever been a son treated like this by his parents? You read about these things in books, but they never really happen. My parents . . . out of a book! They blame me for everything, would you believe it? My father's bad heart they blame on me. My sister's poor grades. When my mother gets in a bad mood, it's my fault. My father's business . . . Me, me, me, it's my fault. The leaky toilet. Have you ever heard of such things? Have you ever heard of such parents? They even blame me for . . . ," I hear him giggle between sobs, "the cat peeing on the rug."

"Fuck it, boy, come over here."

"Are you sure it's OK?"

"Of course it's OK."

And it was OK, at least most of the time. But with Lyle's great talent for dramatizing himself (on two occasions he didn't speak to me for days because he'd thought I'd insulted him), those middle-of-the-night calls could just as easily be over a poem he'd read, a momentary doubt in the Catholic Church, or Shirley ("She didn't even smile when she saw me, man! Can you imagine that? She just walked on up the street!")

Here's Lyle in a bar. As soon as we're seated with our beers in front of us, he shouts loudly, "I say pleasure dilutes happiness," and pours Seven-Up into his beer. No one can say a word while he elaborates his new theory: true happiness consists of long and agonizing suffering. When any of us attempt to interrupt, he yells, "Let ME talk!"

After the first round he turns vindictive. I'm the target. "You! You're always telling me that you're against society. Well, why don't you get out then? You guys are all alike." He's now including everyone at the table, that is, his entire circle of closest friends. "You talk a lot, but you don't do a damned thing. You don't follow your beliefs. Look at me. I hitchhiked to Morgantown. I saw a little of life. I'm out earning my living." He was working for his father. "I make my bread and butter. You guys are all leeches, sponges. What do you do that's useful? When have you had to work? You're all hot air and no action."

He's getting so loud we're in danger of being thrown out, pushing our luck as not one of us has a draft card. As diplomatically as we can, we maneuver him outside and into Joe's car.

I'm in the back seat; he's in the front. He turns around, crawls over the seat, better to shake his accusing finger in my face. "What happened to that three-day trip you were going to take with no money? You don't know anything about life. ALL YOU KNOW IS WHAT YOU READ IN BOOKS!"

But two hours later we're in the back room of the Owl. Lyle is drunk and telling us how much he loves us. "You guys are the only friends I've got. We've got to stick together."

He kept telling us that he was going to quit drinking, but he never did, mixing his beer half and half with Seven-Up, stirring it with his long bony finger, grinning evilly, shouting at us about a new theory, a new idea, a new key to the universe—the one that would finally pull everything together so that it would all make sense. And just as easily as he could end up loving us all, he could end up crying, repeating that no one loved him, no one cared, that he had no friends, no one to understand and appreciate what he knew and how deeply he suffered. All this despite the fact that he would be surrounded by friends, all listening more or less sympathetically, buying him beer, lighting his pipe. And a hundred and one nights he'd get up and leave, to walk home, all the way home, all the way home *alone,* the ten or twenty or thirty blocks home, to punish us for not loving him.

March, 1959

BY THE spring of our junior year, Lyle and I had taken to hitchhiking around, sometimes with a destination in mind, but often enough anywhere at all, just to be going, to have the feeling that we were independent and alone in the world. One night we ended up in St. Stevens, Ohio. We made it in one ride, having been picked up by a maniac who pushed his car down the road at a minimum of a hundred miles an hour; at times he had it up to a hundred and thirty. I'd never gone that fast before and stared, fascinated, at the speedometer. And all the time he was driving, he talked to us out of the corner of his mouth—about his car.

At that time I didn't know a cam shaft from a crank shaft, so I didn't retain much of the driver's lecture about the wonderful mechanisms which were enabling us to tear through the night at such suicidal speed. Only one thing stuck: he said he had an "Isky Roller Cam." That mysterious entity became for me a symbol of the very essence of speed and deadliness in an automobile. At times, when I'd be drunk in a fast car, I'd catch myself chanting it under my breath—"Isky Roller Cam! Isky Roller Cam!"—like an incantation. Even after friends explained to me what it was and how it worked, the phrase lost none of its power, still meant speed and demons and night, not just a piece of metal going around under the hood. We got out in the downtown, what there was of it, and watched the mad driver vanish, his tires screaming. "Isky Roller Cam!" I said. Lyle and I laughed.

So there we were in St. Stevens, at nine o'clock in the evening on Saturday night. It took us all of five minutes to walk the entire length of the main street, from the drugstore on one end to the gas station on the other. "What the hell did we come here for?" Lyle said.

"I'll be damned if I know."

We looked at each other. I don't know what we were expecting, something new maybe, a site of adventure, a town of peasant farmers dancing in the streets, a Babylon complete with Whore. We should have known better. There *were* girls on the street, dressed up for Saturday night and making the rounds in twos and fours; some of them gave us the eye, or so we thought—us, the strangers!—but we were too shy to speak to any of them. We began to walk out of town.

Lyle was talking about Saint Francis, one of the great heroes of his childhood. "The life of that man . . . so pure and dedicated, but with such fervor." He said he wanted to live as Saint Francis had, at a constant pitch of religious excitement and ecstasy. We walked farther into the country, until the sounds of the street traffic faded out altogether. "But he was a man too," Lyle said, "a soldier, a fighting man. He had a wild life. Drinking, women."

"And then he gave it up and turned to God," I said.

"Yes."

"Well, we can do the same thing."

Lyle stopped walking, thought about that for a while. "I think that's heresy," he said. He'd stopped completely still, was rubbing his hands together, appeared lost in thought. Then he looked directly at me. "The important thing is to learn how to live, to live purely, under God's eye. Saint Francis only got there through experience and suffering . . . great suffering. And all that time he was wild, he must have felt some lack in his life that made him turn to God . . . But we have more than that, more than he did. We have his example, for one thing. We don't have to make the same mistakes he made."

"But that's exactly the point," I said, "that he made his own mistakes . . . that he lived through his mistakes and kept on going. That's what we've got to do. Second-hand experience can't be anything but meaningless for us. We've got to cover the same road to get there . . . make our own mistakes. There's no way to make it easy."

"No, no," Lyle said, beginning to walk again. "I can't believe that. I can't. Do we have to do evil before we can do good?"

"Maybe," I said.

"No," quite firmly this time, "that's heresy."

A car was coming down the road. "Shall we?" I said. Lyle nodded. We stuck out our thumbs. The car didn't even slow down.

It was a beautiful night, full of stars and quite warm for that early in the spring. We walked, waved our thumbs at the few cars that passed. Without discussing it, we'd begun to hitchhike back toward Raysburg. Lyle remained lost in thought.

"Maybe we'll get back before the Owl closes," I said. Lyle giggled.

Suddenly he reached out and pounded me on the chest with his fist. "You've got to train," he said.

"What?" I was startled.

He thumped me again. "You've got to TRAIN . . . HARD. You've got to WORK."

I was taken aback. "I have been working," I said.

"Working," Lyle said, snorting, dismissing in that one word all of my efforts to date. "You haven't done anything yet. You've got to TRAIN HARD. That's what you need, John. That's where you'll find it. Work. Suffering. Then when you read those books, you'll know what they're talking about . . . You're going to be good . . . a good miler. Look at that chest on you. You've got it. A good heart. Now you've got to work."

"All right," I said tentatively. Lyle always had the ability to make me believe, at least for as long as I was talking to him, that I could be an athlete. I found the idea appealing, had visions of Lyle and me winning the mile run in the Valley Championship, sweeping in one and two, burying the field—certainly not this year, but maybe next. "What should I do?"

"Run," he said, grinning at me. "Run all the time."

I didn't say anything.

"It's like a rosary," he said. "Every lap is a prayer."

By the time we got back to Raysburg, all the bars had closed.

The night we hitchhiked to St. Stevens changed something for me. It wasn't as though Lyle had said anything new.

Maybe it was being out in the country, in the dark with the stars, or maybe it was that I was finally ready to listen. I don't know. But after that I was serious.

I was reading Plato in those days; the *Symposium* was my favorite dialogue. All those philosophers sprawled around the table drinking wine and looking for *The Truth*—wasn't that just the way we went after it? And when Alcibiades comes stumbling in, plastered, to deliver his speech about the virtues of Socrates, I was completely entranced. Wily Socrates with his annoying questions! Standing for hours thinking, outmarching everyone during Xenophon's campaign, walking barefoot in the snow, drinking all night and then going about his business without bothering to go to bed—there was a true hero. He fit perfectly into Lyle's religion of athletics, into our search for "the way to live." I've never forgotten the Socratic motto: "We will either find what we are seeking or we will free ourselves from the persuasion that we know what we do not know."

I took the mattress off my bed and slept on boards. I stopped using a pillow. I removed the drapes from my windows so the light of dawn would wake me up. I took books from the library on athletics, calisthenics, weight lifting, running. I did push-ups and sit-ups every morning and evening. I put a bar in the door of my bedroom and vowed never to pass through the door without chinning myself. I told my mother that I was in training, to serve me plain meat and salads—no potatoes, please. She was used to my craziness—my "phases" as she put it—and did what I asked without comment. My father said, "What's up, John? You going to go fifteen rounds with Floyd Patterson?" But I could tell that he was pleased with me for a change.

And I ran everywhere I went. Off for an evening with the boys, I'd start running from the front door of my house, all the way up Front Street, across the bridge and into town, stopping only when I had to. I'd meet Lyle on a predetermined corner (he would have just run all the way up from South Raysburg), and we'd stand there panting, sweat pouring down our faces, delighted with each other.

When we ran the mile in practice, I could beat most of the freshmen now, but in real meets, I always finished last. I learned to love track practice though, particularly later in the spring when we finally got a long series of wide blue days full of puffy cumulus clouds. I loved walking around the track with Lyle, talking; I loved warming up and stretching, the calisthenics done in a circle with the coach in the middle; I loved lying on the grass, watching the sprinters at work; I loved the smell of the sawdust in the pole vault and high jump pits, the wintergreen oil we doused all over ourselves until we smelled like an entire pine forest. I even got to the point where, for a moment or two, I almost liked running.

One afternoon, near the end of the season, the coach called the milers. His heart was with his hurdlers, and he never knew what to do with us. "All right," he said, "you guys haven't had much speed work. Today you're going to do a half mile, and I really want to see you put out."

We took off fast. I hadn't gone ten yards when I felt as though I'd grown wings. Lyle—always a fast starter—was leading, and I was catching him, passing everybody to do it. I felt the wind whipping by me on the curve. Something hit me: "So this is what it means to run!" I couldn't believe what was happening, couldn't believe things could be that simple. To run fast, I thought, all you have to do is—run fast.

I passed Lyle at the quarter mile. As I slid by on his right shoulder, he couldn't have looked more surprised if I'd hit him with a pie. I immediately pulled in to the edge of the track, hugging it tight as I'd been taught to do, and kicked for all I was worth. I wasn't running at a middle-distance pace, I was sprinting. I was exploding with joy; I'd found reserves in me I hadn't known were there. I was in love with running. I honestly thought I could keep up that pace forever.

Lyle repassed me, went by without giving me a glance, his jaw rigid, his fists clenched so tight I could see the muscles standing out on his forearms. As I watched him pull away from me, I suddenly felt a wide steel band being wrapped around my chest and cinched in tight. And my lunch on its way up again. But I wasn't a hundred yards from the finish line; I had to do it. I gritted my teeth against the rising vomit and told myself: "Sprint, you fucker." People seemed to be passing me by the hundred. I made it across the finish line before I threw up. Lyle was there to catch me. "What got into you, boy?" he said, laughing. "You were beautiful."

Lyle was having a great season. He was beating everybody in the valley except Alex Warner, Raysburg High's legendary miler, a sullen dark kid with oddly pale eyes. When Warner broke the regional record—Lyle coming in second only a few yards behind him—Lyle clipped the picture of the finish from the *Raysburg Times* and pinned it up above his desk so he would have to see Warner's strained face every time he looked up from his homework. "I want to get to know him," Lyle said.

"Have you ever talked to him?"

"I don't want to *talk* to him. I want to *know* him. Next year I'm going to get that son of a bitch. This is a vow, Dupre. Remember it. Next year's going to be my year."

May, 1959

"END OF the season," Lyle said. We were standing under the showers at the Academy, letting the hot water run over our shoulders. We'd just come back from a meet with Canden High; we'd beaten them soundly. Lyle had won the mile; I'd run it for fun, placed last as usual, but Revington had timed me at 6:22, my best yet. I was pleased with myself. When I'd started the year before, I hadn't even been able to finish a mile. "The last meet always makes me sad," Lyle said. He'd been dawdling around since we got back, as though he didn't want to leave the gym at all.

"There's the Invitational," I said.

"Yeah, but with Warner . . . and those guys from Kiski and Canton . . . I'll be lucky to place at all."

We'd been in the shower so long that the hot water was beginning to run out. I decided to tell him something I'd been thinking about for weeks. "Hey," I said, "there should be girls here."

"What?"

"We should be training with girls, running with girls. There should be girls here right now."

"You're nuts."

"They did it in Sparta."

He giggled, shook his head. "Let's celebrate the end of the season," he said. "Let's get drunk."

Cold beer in the back room of the Pines brought to us by a friendly Polish bartender who didn't ask for our draft cards, that sweet post-run fatigue, rock 'n roll on the jukebox, and all the time in the world to talk. I felt great. I decided to try it again. "Why the hell don't we run with girls?"

"They're different," Lyle said as though repeating a received truth.

"They're not that different."

"Yeah, they are. Too wide in the hips. Haven't got a good stride. Don't have the endurance for long races . . . Besides, why would you want to run with girls?"

"We're too far apart."

"It's just the Academy, boy. That's what it is. You're just horny."

"No, it's more than that. Why is it so goddamned hard?

Why are we so far apart? Not only should we be training with girls, but there should be girls here right now, having a beer with us."

He gave me his sly smile; clearly he thought I was off on one of my mad excursions into Cloud Cuckoo Land. "Would you ever get serious about a girl you could take to a bar?"

"I'm not talking about the way it is. I'm talking about the way it should be."

I'd been reading everything I could about Greek athletics; now I started pouring it all out to Lyle. The Greeks had invented athletics, built the first stadiums; they'd even had showers in their gyms. The Athenians had exercised both their minds and their bodies; Lyle knew that, didn't he? Wasn't it what we'd been saying all along? A sound mind in a sound body? The Olympic Games and Socrates? I told him about Atalanta, the girl runner who'd been so good that not one of the young men in Greece could beat her.

But Lyle wasn't about to be drawn along into my fantasy. "Listen, boy, you're just going to get yourself in trouble thinking like that. That's not the way life is. Girls are different from us."

I knew *that* all right. High heels and lipstick and petticoats, stockings and garter belts, breathy giggly voices, Mom and Dad always hovering in the background—*Be in by ten. No, you can't go to the drive-in. Act like a lady.* The distance from all that to my world of running and sweaty track suits, of bars and beer, of guys who said "fuck" (Fuck you. Fuckin' A, man. What the fuck's happening?) felt enormous, distant as the Dog Star. But I also knew from inside myself—and this was something I could never tell Lyle—just how phony that distance really was. I could have been a girl as easily as a boy, maybe even more easily. When I'd been a little kid, I'd thought half the time that I was really a girl in disguise. So here I was now, a boy convincingly enough, but it was something I'd learned how to do, and what did that say about the supposedly impossible distance between the sexes? I felt as though I had secret information on the subject that I couldn't share with anybody.

"Look," I said, "why can't we just be friends with girls? Why can't we get together just as easily as you and I get together? Why can't we just drop over to see each other without all these goddamned phone calls, and arrangements, and dates?"

Lyle was getting mad at me. "I understand what you're saying, but it's just not possible." Now he was yelling. "If you want to make it with girls, you've got to understand their psychology. You've got to play the game. If you just try to be friends, you'll never get to first base. You'll never get laid. *They're different from us.*"

Different? Oh sure, I certainly did feel that difference, remembered trying to talk to Linda, how goddamned hard it was. But how could she talk to me if she'd never run or got drunk? And how could I talk to her if I'd never worn petticoats or sat around waiting for a phone call? Why couldn't boys be beautiful too? The Athenian boys had shaved off all their body hair, had oiled and powdered themselves. I'd been so clear in my mind only a moment ago, but now I was getting confused. Lyle and I had reached an impasse. I ordered another round of beer. And Lyle was already shifting the subject; he was talking about Shirley, about the Holy Sacrament of Marriage.

The simple happiness I'd been feeling earlier had dissolved. As we got drunker, the world got sadder. We'd been playing the jukebox for over an hour and had finally got it down to one song we were playing over and over: Buddy Holly promising us a love that was surely coming our way. Who was I waiting for? I wondered as I listened to Lyle talk about the joys of a home and family. The Holy Sacrament of Marriage sounded like death to me, but what did I want? What impossible goddess? What saint, what Madonna to resolve the differences, reach across the chasm to me in her infinite mercy, and be everything at once? She'd be as free as a bird, as graceful as a gazelle, as wise as Socrates, and as sexy as an alley cat, both the golden runner of my Greek fantasies and the Bitch Queen I constructed out of the images on the dance floor at the Friday Night Hop, a healthy athlete in stockings and heels, a free thinker in petticoats. I drank until Lyle had to hold me up to get me out the door.

June, 1959

I'VE BEEN pacing back and forth on the wall-to-wall carpet for twenty minutes wondering what could be taking her so long; it's as though I'm marching off an hour of punishment duty. The late afternoon sun slants in the window with a light red as rouge, glints off the antique glass collection. I stare at the picture of Linda dressed as Baby Jane (her description of it), stare outside at the immense lawn that requires a full-time gardener in the summer, fall onto the couch to stare at the oil paintings, the end tables, the goddamned grand piano—everything kept spotless by a maid named Wanda. I don't need to see any more of this; I've memorized it long ago, could draw a diagram accurate down to the placement of the blue Wedgwood candy dish. Finally, I hear Linda's feet on the stairs. Dance-trained, she walks lightly. "Hi, honey." She's got jeans on. I'm so annoyed with her I can't speak.

We've been dating for a year. Her mother won't let her go steady, so she goes out with kids in her own class too, just as I go out with older girls on double dates organized by Revington, who keeps telling me that what I need is "a real woman" (presumably someone like the bitchy, gossipy, not-too-bright Barbara Daniels who's now driving him crazy). But to all intents and purposes, Linda and I *are* going steady; we both know that our dates with other kids don't count. And my friends have certainly *seen* her by now, but I've been careful never to put her in a situation of having to sit down and *talk* to Lyle or any of the others long enough for them to form an impression of her—and judge her. This is to be the first time, the official Junior Class Picnic (as opposed to the unofficial one, all male, which had taken place down at

Fish Creek with kegs of beer and bottles of whiskey), and not only has she kept me waiting forever, but when she does come down, she's dressed wrong, a girl who hardly ever wears pants appearing unexpectedly in jeans, not a skin-tight pair like the trashy Raysburg High girls wear—of course not; she was the Edmonds' darling daughter—but baggy tomboy jeans. Now no one will be able to see her fantastic legs.

My resentment spills out before I can catch it. "When you go out with me, you wear a skirt."

"It's a picnic, isn't it? Isn't this what you're supposed to wear to a picnic?"

I don't answer. With her most brilliantly promising smile, she says, "Oh, but you like your girls in dresses, don't you?"

She's gone upstairs and I'm left waiting again. My nerves are on edge, tight and twanging. We're already late, and we're going to be later. When she comes back, she hasn't merely changed her jeans for a skirt, she's put a dress on, one of her seemingly endless series of blue dresses that match her eyes. Like a World War I general fighting for every inch, she's won half a dozen tiny battles with her mother lately. It's not a little kid's dress; the full skirt's long enough. She's allowed to wear a touch of makeup now and has put on as much as she can get away with: pink lipstick and a hint of mascara. Grinning to me, she pirouettes, showing herself off; her petticoats swirl out. She's wearing nylons and black flats. "Is this what you wanted, John?"

It isn't what I'd wanted, but I can't keep sending her back upstairs to change her clothes. This is ridiculous. She takes me by the hand, leads me into the TV room to announce to her father, "He made me put a dress on," getting a chuckle out of distant old Charlie, then, still dragging me along behind her into the kitchen to say it again in the same amused superior voice to her mother, "He made me put a dress on." Something in me's closed up like a clam, and, driving away, I can't say a word.

"What's the trouble, bubble?"

"Nothing, kitten. Everything's just dandy."

I pull in next to the picnic site at Waverly Park, open the door for her, and there's my whole goddamned class—all the guys with their girlfriends. It's exactly what I'm afraid of: there's not another dress anywhere to be seen. Linda runs up to her pal, Sue Eberhardt (who's wearing sneakers and sexy brief shorts), to say in a voice as bright and carrying as a trumpet: "HE MADE ME PUT A DRESS ON." Sue gives me a veiled sideways stare—something profoundly feminine in that look—and covers her mouth with her hand. Then both she and Linda are hanging onto each other; they've broken up into a fit of giggles. I'm not sure exactly what's happening, but I know they're laughing at me.

Revington's got a flask of bourbon. We step behind a tree for a quick one, and he says in the dry drawling voice of a Southern gentleman, "Tell me, John . . . How did you get her to leave her dolls at home?"

"Stick it in your ear, William."

But Lyle's snowed. "She looks like a princess."

My plans are shot. Now I'm in no mood to show off my

bright little girl to anybody; I just want to be alone with her for a while to try to sort out my confused feelings. She's sitting on a bench with Sue Eberhardt; they're leaning close together, their voices going buzz buzz buzz.

"Linda. Come on."

She jumps to her feet. Sue calls after us, "She obviously knows her master's voice."

Walking into the trees, I say, "My God, is she a bitch. What she needs is a good spanking."

"What about me? Do I need a good spanking?"

"Sure, kitten. That's just what you need."

Suddenly she's kissing me, her open mouth nibbling at mine. I can taste her lipstick. "Will you really do it, John? Will you pull my panties down?" I reach for her, but she's already gone, skipping away. She's put a tree between us, leans around it to say, "But what if I'd laugh?"

"I'd hit you harder."

"What if I'd cry?"

"I don't know what I'd do."

She steps around the tree, slips her arms around me and one of her legs between mine. Her moist tongue slides into my ear. She knows what that does to me, and it's become one of her favorite tricks. Once, under the pretext of whispering something, she'd done it right in her goddamned living room in front of her parents. And now, as I reach for her, she's gone again, laughing. A dumb blistering erection's got me bent nearly double, and by God, I don't know what to do with her *now*.

Hand-in-hand we walk to the playground. I'm on the edge of exploding. She sits down on a swing and kicks off like a child, dazzling me with her smile as she always does. When she swings forward, her skirt and petticoats are swept back, revealing her long smooth legs to the tops of her nylons, then, at the end of the arc, her skirt closes like a blossom. Her small feet are arched and pointed like a ballerina's. I've gone beyond anything as simple as mere sexual arousal— an ache that starts in my prick and balls and gradually spreads up through my belly and chest and into my throat, a miserably keen throbbing timed to that swing. Damn it, I should have kept my mouth shut about the jeans. She's defeated me again, and I can never figure out exactly how she does it.

I TOOK a lot of shit from some of the boys about Linda (but never from Lyle who believed that love had nothing to do with volition, but rather was something that fell on you out of the sky like a meteorite). Later, the kidding gradually changed to a grudging acceptance—by our senior year to outright envy. Linda turned out to be as stunning as her mother.

"I'm beginning to think you had the right idea all along, ace," Revington told me sourly after one of his repetitious fights with Barbara. "You get them young and then you can train them."

Looking back, I think that my pet name for her was more apt than I knew at the time: like a kitten, she might have been cute, but she had claws too. Both of us were more complex than the time would let us be easily, and now I'm trying to see all the facets of her. Everybody had always told her that high school was much harder than grade school, and she kept waiting for it to get hard, but it never did. One of her facets was that of a conventional "good girl"; she did her homework diligently every day and got straight A's. Her sophomore year she was asked by her gung-ho biology teacher if she wanted to join a small group of honors students—all boys—and dissect a rat instead of the lowly frog the rest of the class was doing. To my surprise, she jumped at the chance. No, it didn't bother her, she said. He was a big fat white rat, and the kids named him Fred. They pinned him down on a board under a fluorescent light, pared away at him with a surgeon's knife, and drew diagrams of his various systems with colored pencils. She came home from school stinking of formaldehyde. "It's really fun," she told me. "A mammal's much more interesting than an amphibian." By the time she finished, she'd examined Fred Rat from tail to snout, knew every twist and sinew of his anatomy; her drawings covered twenty pages.

But to be so nonchalant about poor old Fred, she could be amazingly finicky about other things. Gym class for instance. "I really hate it. All those girls running around and sweating. Everything smells like old tennis shoes and dirty socks." I was amazed to find out that she didn't like ballet all that much either. I saw her in only one recital. In stage makeup, pointe shoes, and tutu—the full length of her legs on display—she seemed to me nearly the refined quintessence of sexiness, but "I'm not that good," she told me, and, the year she turned fifteen, quit. "It's too much time and work unless you want to be a professional dancer." She and her mother fought about it for weeks.

"She blames it on you," she told me wryly.

"On me?" I didn't want her to quit. I thought ballet was the perfect thing for her.

"She blames everything on you."

I suppose it's amazing that we were allowed to be together as much as we were; at the time it seemed only our natural right. In memory, I'm always talking, stuck, pacing up and down in her kitchen or living room, talking—holding hands and strolling with her by the creek, talking. I hear my voice going on and on—about life, suffering, poetry, Nietzsche, Jack Kerouac—and I see her huge lovely eyes looking at me. As I begin to learn folk tunes, accompanying myself painfully on the guitar, I sing them to her while she listens patiently. As I worry about which colleges to apply to, what to do with my life, how I'm ever going to learn to be a writer—I tell her all about it. I see her charming, little-girl smile and eyes bright as sunrise. I think now that the reason it's so hard to remember much of what she said back to me (beyond a handful of words that persist sharply cut as crystal beads) is that I didn't give her a chance to say much of anything.

For her fifteenth birthday, I gave her *Civilization and Its Discontents*. Her mother gave it back to me, saying, "I think Linda's too young for this, John."

EVENTUALLY I had to take Linda home to meet the old man—to meet my mother too, of course, but, even though I kept telling myself I hated his guts, I knew that he was the one who counted. Linda must have picked up my anxiety by osmosis; she dressed perfectly—not either too young or too sexy—in a full-skirted dress and no makeup at all. My mother focused on one tiny incident and wouldn't let go; she must have repeated a hundred times, "That young lady has real manners. She stood up when I walked into the room. How many girls these days would know to do that?" It seemed to me an asinine thing to be the basis of an entire character analysis—that moment when Linda rose gracefully to her feet—but there it was, and for my mother everything else followed with an eerie logic: Linda was a nice girl; she would not get me into trouble, not lead me off onto any crooked paths, not want to get married at eighteen. Looking back on it, I've come to understand that my mother's screwy assessment was absolutely accurate.

Linda sent my father spinning off into his full-blown lady's-man routine; the words poured out of his mouth like molasses. He complimented me on my good taste in women. He noticed that Linda's dress matched her eyes and complimented her on that. He told her that she had the most beautiful eyes he'd ever seen in his life. Teasingly, he offered her a drink. She turned on him the full million watts of her heart-stopping smile and said, "Oh, Mr. Dupre, you know I'm not old enough to drink."

He sat down six inches away from her, dragging a chair

three feet to do it, leaned into her face with his own glass of bourbon in his hand, and told her he'd bet she was old enough to do lots of things. Not flustered in the least, she said nothing to that unanswerable remark, but cocked her head to one side and kept on smiling. When she stood up to leave, he told her, "With legs like that, you should be in pictures. Betty Grable's got nothing on you, kid."

In the car she said, "Your father's cute." I said nothing. I thought he was a pain in the ass.

I was usually careful to avoid running into the old man in the kitchen at two in the morning on Saturday nights, but I couldn't always manage it. One night he stumbled in to catch me right in the middle of constructing a sandwich. I was drunk as a lord, but my father was drunker. He steadied himself with a hand on the wall, leered at me out of a sweaty beet-red face; he smelled as though he'd practically drowned in whiskey. "Getting into that high-class little piece yet?" he said.

I was shocked down to my toenails. Fathers do not say things like that to their sons; it was unthinkable. So I said back to him what sons aren't supposed to say to their fathers: "For Christ's sake, Dad. Jesus."

Chuckling obscenely, winking as though he'd developed a facial twitch, he lurched off to bed, leaving me with, "When I was your age, I'd already got a girl in trouble."

A year or so later I cornered him—both of us sober— and reminded him of what he'd said that night. Blandly, flatly, without a ripple on his face, he denied having said any such thing.

DURING OUR senior year, something strange began to happen to Lyle. The first symptom of it was that he didn't go out for football. He'd never been one of the stars of the team by any means, but he'd played first string, and the coach—known to us as "the Bull"—couldn't understand it. The Bull wasn't much for understanding anything; the way he let the guys know that he thought they'd been dogging it in practice was to sneak into the locker room at night and put bouquets of pansies in their helmets. According to Lyle (I didn't necessarily believe him), the Bull had jumped up and down when he'd heard about it, had torn at what was left of his hair. Lyle claimed that all he'd said back to the coach—repeated firmly—had been: "I'm in serious training for the mile."

Lyle had been running all summer; he was up to ten miles of road work at a clip, and he didn't want to let it go. What he wanted was an undefeated track season, Alex Warner's regional record—and Alex Warner's ass on a plate. He'd still go to the bars with us, but he'd drink only Seven-Up. While the football team practiced in the center of the field, Lyle ran around the perimeter of it, a one-man track team. Every weekend he took to the roads. He'd always been thin, but now he began to look cadaverous. His bunched knotty muscles stood out like wood carvings; stripped down, he could have been used for a living anatomy lesson.

Long-distance running was relatively unexplored terrain in the fifties. Now we know that hours of road work tightens up the backs of the legs like watch springs, that runners must stretch as routinely and carefully as ballet dancers, but Lyle never stretched anything, and by early winter he was suffering from a number of ailments that now would be called "overuse syndromes." He had recurring shin splints, Achilles tendonitis, lower back pains. He regarded all these difficulties the way Saint Anthony probably regarded his demons, recounted every ache and agony to us with obvious enjoyment. "My God, did it hurt! But it didn't stop me." He didn't go out for basketball either; he planned to run right through winter and into the spring. And, of course, nobody back then had discovered another phenomenon now known as "runner's insomnia."

Lyle saw his inability to sleep as merely an additional temptation to be overcome. After an hour or two of thrashing around in bed, he'd get up, pull on his sweats, and take off. He'd run from home all the way up to 23rd Street where the whorehouses were. It eased his mind, he said, to look at the whorehouses. They were closed by the time he got there (two or three in the morning), so there was no question of his going in. He just walked, and looked, and ran home again. And then would get up at seven to come to school. Under the drawn skin of his face, the bone of his skull showed through like a *memento mori;* his eyes glittered like gemstones. The guys were beginning to whisper behind his back: "Lyle's going nuts."

The snow wasn't going to stop him, by God. He'd always run in snow; it made training more efficient, he said, gave you more work for the time you put in. On the high steep hills behind his house, the snow piled up and persisted. Lyle chopped his way up, sometimes floundering to his waist. At the top he'd kneel and pray to his favorite saints to make him worthy of the regional record. And it was the snow that finally did him in. One Monday he wasn't in school. By Wednesday I was worried and called his house; his father told me that Lyle couldn't come to the phone, but over the weekend Lyle called me, asked me to bring his homework to him.

In a hoarse, quivering voice he said, "I'm giving it all up, John. I'm going to join the Trappists."

"What the hell are you talking about, boy?"

"The doctor says I've got pneumonia."

LYLE'S ROOM was in the attic; it suited him perfectly. Under the low sloping ceilings he'd crammed in several cases of books, his ham radio with a statuette of Saint Francis on top, his telescope and microscope, various test tubes and bottles, strange electronic devices, his rock and fossil collection, some boxes of dirt in which nasturtium plants were proving by their absence that they did not take well to being doused with acetic acid, and his bed, desk, and clothes. On the walls were a picture of Jesus with bloody heart exposed, a massive black crucifix, and a framed picture of the Saint Stanislaus Grade School Football Team of 1954 from which Lyle, in full football regalia, stared out into the room from an absurdly childish face.

Lyle lay in his narrow bunk bed wrapped up in quilts.

He looked like Lazarus. On a blackboard directly next to him he'd chalked up, in huge block letters: REMEMBER DEATH.

I sat with his homework assignments on my lap; neither he nor I gave a shit about his homework. "What the hell's that?" I said, pointing to the blackboard.

"The only words the Trappists are allowed to speak," he said. "Otherwise they maintain total silence."

"All right, what's this about the Trappists?"

"I'm going to join the order as soon as I graduate," he said grimly. "Their clothes are their shrouds, and they sleep in their coffins." His voice sounded as though he'd been reciting those words over to himself; now that he had a chance to speak them out loud, he couldn't help smiling. "I forgot my curse," he said. "It's the only way I can expiate it."

Of course he'd told me about his curse; it had been one of the high points of his life. He'd whispered the story to me in the back room of the Pines after closing time; it wasn't something he'd talk about sober, in the daylight.

Lyle dreamed away most school nights in the Ohio County Public Library, doing his homework, falling in love—at a distance—with the giggling girls, writing poems to them in his notebook. He could run there in twenty minutes, and it was a quiet place where he could get away from his family. In the summer, I could always find him there late on Saturday afternoons. He would have run in the mornings; at night he'd have a date with Shirley lined up, or a drinking bout with me, so all that was left of the day to kill would be those last few tedious hours—reading *Sports Illustrated* or browsing through the stacks marked "religion." It'd happened last July; he'd stepped out of the library into a perfectly ordinary sunny afternoon and had seen the old Negro woman sitting across the street on the steps of the Baptist Church. She was a fixture there—all of us had seen her at one time or another—so old and wrinkled and brown it was impossible to guess her age, her head wrapped in a bandanna, her feet in floppy shoes with the sides cut out. Along with the retarded Hackett family and strange Davey, "The Moon Dance Man," she was one of the town characters. Everyone said she was a witch.

As Lyle started home toward South Raysburg, he saw that she was following along opposite him on the other side of the street. When he stopped, she stopped. When he began to walk again, so did she. She touched him right in the center of his wild streak of Polish mysticism. He walked faster. She walked just as fast, slapping along in her old cracked shoes. Finally, in a panic, he turned and stared at her. She immediately crossed the street, walked directly up to him, and spat in his face. "You are cursed," she screamed. He made the sign of the cross and ran all the way home.

Now I looked at his tired face and tried to figure out if he was serious about his curse or only assuming another of his self-dramatizing poses. His illness showed; his skin looked like yellow parchment. "Have you talked to anybody about this?" I said.

"Of course I have." He stared down his nose at me; his

tone of voice said: What do you think I am, an idiot?

"Who? Your priest?"

"My confessor, yes"

"What did he say?"

"He suggested I join the Trappists."

So that was it. "Was he serious?"

"He thinks I have a vocation."

"So do I. You're going to break the regional record in the mile run."

"No, that's over now. It's *all* over." I saw by his faint smile that he was enjoying himself thoroughly.

"What about Shirley and the Holy Sacrament of Marriage?"

"That's over too. It's not for me."

I knew he was just as hungry for sex as I was, and I would have taken bets that it was precisely that hunger which would keep him out of any monastic order without additional help from me. I also believed in his crazy holiness, so I was only half kidding when I said, with my face perfectly straight, "Pray for me, Lyle."

"I do, John. I pray for you, and myself, and all of us."

April, 1960

GREEN DAYS. "Jesus, it's been a hard year." Lyle and I are jogging gently around the track with our sweats on. The vivid spring sky is jogging too, rolling out over our heads, wind and rain still miles away, but we can smell it, feel the tingle of it: warm, green, electric, and inevitable.

"Jesus, I feel great . . . Isn't it wonderful to be happy and know it right when it's happening? Not for it to be something you have to look back on and remember? Well, I'm happy *right now.*"

Lyle punches me lightly on the shoulder. "We going to whip their asses down at Harrod, or what?" he says, turning my words back into running.

It's all right with me. "Yeah, boy, we're going to whip their asses."

"Four-forty," the coach is yelling. A big man, his voice booms out across the field. He yawns and stretches, touches his toes; the stop watch around his neck swings like a pendant. "Hey, coach, you can't run very fast on Friday," somebody yells. The coach laughs.

Lyle's made an amazing recovery from his illness of last winter, but he's still nowhere near where he used to be. All the work he did before he got sick has improved his speed remarkably. He was always fast; now he has a sprint that can bury everybody but our very best dash men, but the effect of the pneumonia shows in the last quarter of the mile. There Lyle ties up, bogs down, suffers. He hasn't come even close to five minutes yet this season, but he's surprisingly cheerful about it. He no longer talks about Alex Warner and the regional record; now he's obsessed with *his comeback,* and he's sure it will come back—that lost endurance—fall upon him like grace and push him on to victory sometime before the season's out. He hasn't mentioned the Trappists in months, he's talking again about marrying Shirley, and he refers to his parish priest as an idiot: "That man doesn't know a thing. The Church is big enough for everybody . . . even you." I can't quite figure out where he's gone; all I know is that he's once again fun to be with. He's drinking again too, and he always tells me at least once each time we're loaded: "I know you, Dupre. There's only one place for you. You'll die in the Church."

The coach calls the mile run. Lyle and I lace up our spikes. "My, my, my," Lyle says, rubbing his hands together. He looks at me out of the corner of his eye. "You're going under six today."

"Oh, am I?"

"Damned straight. Harrod's only got two milers that are worth anything, so if you can get under six, you'll place. We'll need that point."

"All right, I'll try it."

"I'll pace you. All you have to do is stay with me, and I'll pull you under." I grin at him. The spring of our senior year is so wonderful that I believe I can do it.

We line up at the start. I've been running for three years, and it's changed me. I'm still not a genuine miler and know it, but at least now I can stride through the distance in good form. I've knocked a minute off my time, but I've never gone under six.

"Runners take your marks," the coach says.

"Vladimir Kuts," Lyle tells me. "Just tick it off easy, click, click, click."

We're running, and I've taken the lead. It's too fast, but I don't care. At the quarter, Eddie Pachinka whips by me—"Keep at it, Johnny"—and is gone down the track. Lyle slides in next to me, and we hit the half just under three. "See how easy it is," he says, but I'm gutting it out now, a breath for every stride, sweat in my eyes. "Stretch it out, stretch it out." Lyle's voice is soft, crooning. "Long, long, long stride. Remember Bannister." Right. To run the mile, Bannister said, you've got to hit the tape with nothing left, not even enough to keep you standing upright. My mind says no, I can't possibly do it, but my body says fuck you. My body wants to run. It's April, and in a couple months I'll be out of high school forever. An invisible cord ties me to Lyle's elbow; we sail by the coach, watch in his hand, who yells after us: "Five fifty-five."

"Oh how easy," Lyle says, but I can't breathe. He slips an arm over my shoulders, and we keep on walking. "Let's do a slow two and some wind sprints."

I can speak again. "It's Friday, boy. I'm going up to Linda's."

Usually I could walk from the Academy to her house in half an hour, but that day I took my time, babying my legs. I hadn't seen her in two weeks, the longest it had been since we'd started going together—hadn't called her either. We'd had our first serious fight, but now it seemed trivial. I was so full of myself—under six, by God, about to graduate with honors, by God—that I was sure I could convince her it was trivial too. The anguished boy who'd sat up in bleak winter nights writing Nietzschean poems about struggle and pain and death seemed to be somebody else. Maybe I'm growing up, I thought.

I caught Linda in one of those moments that you want to keep forever like a good photograph. I walked up the steps to the kitchen and paused just outside the screen door. She hadn't heard me coming, was sitting at the table with a school book open in front of her, a glass of milk and a couple peanut butter cookies on a saucer. She was reading without any lights on, and the stormy daylight made her skin look as pale and iridescent as a frog's belly seen under water. She had a face that needed to be rediscovered. In just a few days I'd forgotten the complex beauty of it, but now I was stopped. Feeling something like awe, I stared at her. It was the first time I was consciously aware that I was in love with her—not only in love but so deeply committed that everything else in my life felt insignificant.

She turned a page in her book, frowned at it. Loving her seemed to be enabling me to see her truthfully: too thin to be anybody's pin-up, breasts too small, nose too long and straight. (Damn it, I thought, she does look like a dog.) She was wearing a simple blouse, a pleated skirt, and nylons, her long legs crossed under the table, the shoes she'd worn to school that day—brown heels—resting neatly side by side next to her chair. She wasn't an easy beauty like her mother; she had to work at it, and I loved that in her—her plainness and her effort to be something else—loved her collie nose and alabaster skin so sensitive to the sun that she had to wear, in the summer, a broad-brimmed hat, loved her narrow shoulders, slender wrists, and long white neck. I knocked on the door. She jumped as if something had stung her.

No bouncy bright chatter today. "Oh," she said flatly, "did you get lost?"

"No."

"I thought maybe you did. Come in."

"No, you come out. Come for a walk with me."

"You're an idiot. It's going to rain."

"That's all right."

She looked at me a moment, the screen door between us, then shrugged. "All right." I waited while she went upstairs. She came back with loafers in her hand, sat down and put them on. "Hey, Mom," she called, "John's here. We're going for a walk."

From somewhere in the huge house, "It's going to rain, Linda."

"Oh, Mother, for heaven's sake!" She pushed past me out the door. "Well, are we going?"

We walked down the hill to the little footbridge above the creek. She wouldn't let me hold her hand. She didn't say a word.

We'd been at a party at Sue Eberhardt's, and I'd thought she'd been paying a bit too much attention to a tall blond guy from Canden High named David Anderson, had said something to her about it. What had really rasped at me had been her choice: Canden's only halfway decent miler. "We're not going steady, John," she'd said, "and even if we were, I can still

72

talk to other boys, can't I?" Later that night I'd gone to get her a Coke, had come back and found her sitting on the couch with him. I'd kept right on going out the front door. She'd come after me. "What's the matter with you? Don't be such a baby." I hadn't answered, had continued walking to the car determined to make a dramatic exit—somewhat difficult with a useless Coke in each hand. "You ass," she'd yelled after me. Thinking about it now, it seemed one of the stupidest things I'd ever done in my life.

We leaned on the railing of the footbridge and looked down into the creek below, swollen with spring run-off, racing with water. The air was prickly with the coming rain. "I love days like this," I said.

"Oh sure," she said sarcastically. She'd slipped the gold charm bracelet off her wrist and was dangling it over the railing, twisting the chain nervously in her fingers.

"Kitten . . .? I'm sorry."

She was standing with her back arched, her hips cocked, the lines of her lovely girl's bottom showing clearly under her skirt, her legs in glossy stockings pressed tightly together at the knee. It was a very sexy posture. "You make me sick," she said.

I didn't say anything. The bracelet ran between her fingers with a quickly iridescent motion like a garter snake in long grass and was gone into the creek. It lay between the shiny pebbles, water running over it, and for a moment she looked like a child about to cry.

"Get it for me," she said, and then laughed. "I certainly

am a spoiled brat sometimes, aren't I?"

I took off my shoes and socks, rolled my pants up, and waded out for it. Despite the warmth of the day, the water was like ice. She held out her hand for me, and I slipped the bracelet over her wrist. "It's too loose," she said. I put my shoes back on.

We were looking into each other's eyes; hers were blue and angry. "If you ever walk out on me again, that's the end."

I shrugged.

"You idiot," she said, "I was just teasing you." I caught her around the waist and tried to kiss her, but she dug her thumbs into my ribs. "Don't. Stop it." We stared at each other, deadlocked. The rain began to come down in drops fat as quarters.

We were both thinking the same thing—the gazebo. Before I'd met her, I'd never heard the word, and I still couldn't understand why anybody would build a little round open-air room with a pointed roof on it smack out in the middle of their back lawn, even if their back lawn did cover almost an acre. I made it first; she jumped in a moment behind me, shook the water out of her hair. She slipped easily into my arms, kissed me, her tongue between my lips, but pulled away, walked to the other side of the gazebo and looked down the hill toward the creek, leaving me with an aching hollow space where she'd been.

The happiness I'd been feeling was blown now like one of my mother's Debussy runs. I sat down on the circular bench in the center of this dopey little building; the rain was hammering the roof. I was so confused I couldn't even put together the right question: something about Linda as impossible as a boulder. And then she did the most provocative thing she'd ever done to me (and she'd done plenty). In a quickly graceful movement, as though mounting a horse, she sat down on my lap, facing me, straddling me, her skirt pushed up to her waist, exposing the white garters that held up her nylons. Her panties were white too, were pushed firmly against the buttoned fly of my uniform pants. I was instantly as erect as I could be, trapped as I was under layers of tight cloth. She linked her hands behind my neck and stared at me; her expression mirrored my own puzzled and exasperated feelings. I caught and stopped myself just before saying what I'd never said to her: "I love you, Linda." Instead I sat and held her.

"John," she said, "I'm only fifteen."

"You'll be sixteen in two months."

"I know when my birthday is." I couldn't understand why she sounded so angry.

GREEN EVENINGS. Harrod is a small school down-state; we're the visiting team. They have one miler consistently under five minutes, and some good weight men, a few good sprinters, but not much depth. "They'll take a lot of firsts," Lyle says, "but we'll clean up everything else."

Cool spring air, country air, and stadium lights so we'll be able to see later, but we don't need them now; the sun hasn't quite set into twilight. Lyle and I walk around the field in our sweat suits. "This could be the one," he says and punches me on the shoulder. "You've got to do it. We're going to need that point." I say nothing. I've run in every meet this season and never placed. I know that this could be the one, know that we're going to need the point, and I'm scared to death.

I follow Lyle on a quick tour of the field events. We're doing all right in the discus and the jumps, but in the shot, all we've got left is Kupla, and unless he comes up with the best throw of his life, the best we can hope for is a third. Worst of all, Revington is already out of the pole vault, has failed at some ridiculously low height. He's walking off the field, passes us with a jaunty salute. "Sorry, gentlemen, not my night."

"Asshole," Lyle says to Revington's receding back. "It's never his night."

By the time they call the mile run, night is closing carefully over the stadium like a cupped palm. In the west a painful blue, like spilled ink, streaks the sky; the huge lights are gathering mist and insects into them, and, even though I've warmed up, I suddenly feel chilled to the core. Fear has heightened my mind to a frantic blurring of wordless pictures. I slap pungent wintergreen oil onto my legs. When the coach hands me a pill, my hand's shaking so badly I can hardly take it. The pill says 4, the number of my lane.

Lyle's next to me in lane three. "Don't try to keep up with me," he says under his breath. "Run it even. Stay with the pack. Kick it home." It's the same thing he tells me every meet. Harrod's runners are lining up with us. Our colors are gold and black; theirs are blue. I feel the ritual, the heraldry, of this, wish desperately that I could live up to it, live up to what Lyle wants me to do, live up to every runner in our school—past, present, and future.

The Academy only has three runners entered. Since Lyle's never quite recovered from his pneumonia, Eddie Pachinka has become our best miler. He's steady, dependable. Every time he runs, no matter how stiff or slack the competition, no matter the temperature, state of the track, or importance of the meet, he runs a five-minute mile. He's lucked out and drawn the inside lane. And Harrod's also entered only three runners. They give points for five places. I've got to beat just one of them to place, and the team scores are so close that it's going to count. Lyle knows what I'm thinking and gives me a grin. "Run it, boy," he says. "Run it good."

"Runners take your marks." I fall automatically into a crouch; my mind is one enormous smear of panic. The gun goes off, and we're off, Lyle rabbiting away as though he's planning to drop out after the first quarter, and right behind him two of their runners, then Pachinka. Their third man falls in behind at a moderate pace, and I'm right on his heels.

At the quarter Lyle is breaking their asses, must be close to sixty seconds. Pachinka knows damned well that Lyle isn't going to keep up that insane pace. He's seen Lyle do it too many times before, take off like a maniac only to come limping in at the finish like one of Napoleon's soldiers stumbling back from the Russian Front, so Pachinka just runs steadily, aimed at his five-minute mile. But the front runners don't know anything about Lyle, and they're trying to keep up with him. It's hurting them; I can see it. And I'm hurting myself because, even though I'm sixty yards back of Pachinka by now, I'm still sticking to their third man, and I've never run the first quarter of a mile this fast before.

At the half the field is spreading out like a fan, Lyle still leading, with one of their guys determined to stay with him. Then, a long way back, is their second runner, in trouble and working hard. Then much farther away, Pachinka, relaxed and running beautifully. And I'm still with their third man, although I don't think I've ever been in such pain in my life. Panting through a mouthful of sand, lungs straining like toy balloons blown to the edge of bursting. Stomach full of ground glass, a knife in the side, and a dangerous twinge of nausea.

At three quarters I can just barely make out what's happening in the distance, can still distinguish our black and gold from their blue, can see Lyle's distinctively knotty body begin to wobble with fatigue. He's suckered their best two runners and destroyed them, and probably himself right along with them. Pachinka, looking fresh enough to keep on going to Pittsburgh, moves easily past everyone and into the lead. Harrod's front runner has dropped back, stumbling like an amputee. His teammate has passed him and is catching up with Lyle now. Lyle glances back over his shoulder at that approaching figure, and I have enough mind left to wonder if he imagines himself as Landy with Bannister coming on strong. And then, suddenly, Lyle takes off as though he's been kicked in the ass.

So what do I do? I pass their last man. Just the way it says to do it in the track books, just the way Lyle has told me a thousand times to do it—I pull up to his shoulder as he's coming into a curve, sneak on by him, sprint away, and try to look fresh as a galloping pony, though I'm feeling like a damned fool. The nausea in my belly is rising into my throat. It's frightening. I'm sure I can't run at that pace much longer without throwing up.

I don't know what happens to the other runners, but later I'll learn that Lyle, although he's tying up badly and groaning aloud with every step, kicks it home to win with his best time of the season—4:48. Pachinka and their best man duel it out for second, Pachinka just edging him at the finish, both under five minutes. Now they've got the third and fourth places, and that leaves nobody on the track but their last man—*and me.* I'm doing the best I can, but I hear the bastard right behind me like the Hound of Heaven in that poem Lyle likes to recite. Footfalls and breathing: bang bang, pant pant, bang bang. And it just hurts too much, that's all there is to it. Why am I doing this to myself? I'm going to slow up and let him pass me and fuck it—fuck the extra point, fuck what Lyle wants me to do, fuck trying to prove anything, fuck it all.

Then something happens. There are times when there isn't any choice, and there isn't any choice because you're an animal. You can put things between yourself and that fact forever, put newspapers and safe houses there, television sets and your parents and friends, put all your masks and social roles there, but a time will come when it's you alone in your animal flesh, with blood pounding, sweat flowing, cells changing—animal that will die. Then it will be no use to say, "OK, I'll forget it, go to a movie or read a book or call somebody up." You won't be able to put it off because you'll be stuck with it, animal. And fighting against dying must be like that. My father's last words, dying, in the white hospital, unable to pretend any longer to be anything other than an animal would be (and this is perfect): "I can't breathe."

And I can't breathe, not very well, running. But I have to do it. Not for Lyle. Not for my team. Not to defeat the guy behind me. Not even for my own ego. No, I have to do it only so I will know that it's possible to do it. I keep on. And he does not pass me. And I take fifth. When I cross the finish line, I start to fall, but Lyle is there to catch me. I am in his bony arms. I smell his sweat and my own sweat. He's holding me in his arms, and he's crying.

"We did it," he says. "We did it together." I don't know what he's talking about; I am dazed. Then it begins to press in on me: he means his win—his comeback!—and my fifth place; he means that after all the talk and visionary nights of our friendship, we've finally placed together in a mile run. I'm glad for his happiness even though he's already turning it into metaphor, even though I myself am already beginning to turn it into metaphor. We walk away, across the field, and there is no position I can find for my body that is comfortable, just ache, shaking muscles, a mouthful of filth, knotted stomach. I hurt all over, and I have never been so happy in my life.

When we got back to the Academy that night, I knew that I had to go straight to Linda. As I climbed the hill to her house, delighting in the pain in my legs, I felt as high and unlimited as the night hawks I could hear in the sky far above me. I was already missing the point; at eighteen, I would have needed to be as wise as Socrates not to miss the point. I was planning what to say to her: *Lyle won and I placed. We beat them. I did the best mile of my life. Revington timed me at* 5:42. I walked across the newly mown lawn, up the back stairs to the yellow light of the safe kitchen. Linda came to me in a plaid dress, smiling, aproned from washing the dishes, and let me take her into my arms. And by then the metaphor had won; I'd let it loom large, take over, settle into weight and importance. My mind was already full of all of those lying words that hadn't meant a thing—*when I'd been running.*

WE HADN'T exactly turned into pals, but I'd never felt easier with my father in my life. I took the *Raysburg Times* sports page and slapped it down in front of him at the breakfast table, pointed to my name: Mile Run, Fifth Place. He looked up at me, grinning ear to ear. I felt a long-awaited triumph; both of us knew that I was going to turn out to be all right after all. I showed it to my mother, and she nodded— "Yes, that's nice, honey"—and drifted off to other things. Whatever I'd wanted had usually been all right with her. When, as a child, I'd decided to be a girl and had wanted to dress like one, that had been all right with her just so long as no one saw me doing it. When, at twelve, I'd wanted to spend every day of the summer in my room reading science fiction, that had been all right too, and so had my recent attempt to turn myself into the perfect Socratic athlete. Years later, when I would come sneaking back to my father's death-bed, traveling under an assumed name, to tell her, "I can't stay for the funeral. The FBI always picks up the guys who come home for funerals," she'd nod at me as though what I'd said was just ordinary common sense. I used to think that she was the personification of kindness; then, later, I revised that to imagining her as totally indifferent, her mind always on something else, and me with never a clue what that might be. But one night when she came up to see me graduate from university, she got drunk, and my mother was never a drink-ing woman. Two gin and tonics went straight to her head, and she said, "I used to worry a lot about you, John. I used to ask myself what I might have done to make you so strange. But then I decided that I hadn't done anything. You would have been strange no matter what I did."

Her family never approved of my father. I've looked at pictures of them back five generations: sternly bearded men, massive women in death-defying corsets, not a smile to be seen. They were British stock, staunch Presbyterians, as laconic as Calvin Coolidge; unbending, ungiving, their motto must have been, "the Lord helps him who helps him-self." Grandfather Wheelright had fought for the Union, and my mother had his discharge papers to prove it. I saw that side of my family only on state occasions; ancient figures pressed nickels into my sweaty hands.

My father's kin, not his family, but his *people,* were spread out through Ohio, Kentucky, and West Virginia on either side of the Ohio River: a red-faced sweet-talking story-telling drunken crew of men; a gaggle of gossipy thigh-slapping women. I was the fourth John Henry Dupre; the first was said to have fled Louisiana after killing a man. "In a gun fight," my father had always told me.

"Nope," says Uncle O. E. Dupre, "it was a knife fight."

"I don't think he killed anybody," my grandmother says. "I think that's just a story."

There are a dozen Dupres in the room, several of them so old I can't imagine why they don't die before my eyes. I'm ten or eleven, fascinated, trying to make sense of all this talk, but the Dupres can't agree on anything. "Well, anyway, he rode with Morgan," my father says, banging his fist on the table. The level in the bourbon bottle is dropping fast.

"Which Morgan was that?"

"The Confederate general. You know . . . What was his name?"

"Billy Morgan."

"No, his name wasn't Billy Morgan. It was Morgan Morgan."

"That's ridiculous. Wasn't anybody named *Morgan* Morgan. And Grandpa Dupre didn't ride with the Morgans anyway. He was a close friend to the Morgans. Went into business with them."

"No, he never went into business with them. They was never in business to start with. But didn't one of the Dupres marry one of the Morgan girls?"

"Wasn't on the Dupre side. That was Grandpa Shenk who founded all of Shenkstown. He married Morgan Morgan's oldest daughter."

"Damn it," my father says, "Grandpa Dupre did ride with the Morgans. He told me so himself."

My grandmother can't let that one pass. "Why, honey, he was dead long before you was born."

"I know it for a fact," my father says, fire in his eyes. "After Grandpa Dupre killed that man in Louisiana, he came up to Kentucky and signed up with the Morgans. Rode with them all through the war. It was *Calvin* Morgan he rode with."

From the stories I heard as a child, I gathered that the Dupres must have lived in a world totally unlike any I had ever seen—a wild and woolly land in which hoop snakes rolled down the road in perfect circles, holding their tails between their fangs; fire balls made of compressed lightning, without any warning, came blazing out of fireplaces; wildcats imitated the cries of newborn babies so accurately that lone women were lured out of their cabins to be eaten up; in the outhouses, sulfur spiders big as saucers glowed in the dark; and someone named Morgan, with a drawn saber in one hand and a gallon demijohn of moonshine in the other, galloped through the night with my great grandpappy by his side, striking terror into the hearts of every man, woman and child north of the Mason–Dixon Line.

But for all the fabulous yarns my father loved to tell about the Dupres running wild somewhere out in the mythic hills of West Virginia, he was a classic Raysburg boy, and I can't imagine him anywhere else than in that wide-open sin-soaked river town. He played poker, played the numbers, bet on everything you could bet on—from the horses and high school football games to the World Series and the Heavyweight Championship of the World. He knew every obscure private club in Center Raysburg and, at one time or another, had got drunk with every shady character in town. He grew up in the twenties; I see him as a sheik from an ancient cartoon—roadster, raccoon coat, and patent leather hair, learning how to dress like a man of means, how to sweet-talk the ladies. Speakeasies, roadhouses, bootleggers, hot bands, fast women: all I heard were bare hints of it. "If I hadn't met your mother, I would have burned myself out like that trumpet player . . . What's his name?" And my mother would smile and say, "Bix Beiderbecke, dear." But she had been the most beautiful of all. "A princess, a queen," he called her. And my mother would add with one of her rare flickers of humor, "A queen working as a salesgirl in Eberhardts' basement."

He was a good businessman at first, then later a bad one as it all fell away from him. "Your dad could always talk anybody out of anything," my mother used to tell me. He spent a fortune on clothes. He said in all seriousness, "Clothes make the man." And when I went away to WVU, that's what drove him crazy—my beatnik grubbiness, my ratty beards, my torn and unwashed jeans, my run-down cowboy boots. "A hillbilly," he called me. "You look just like some hick kid just down out of the hills who's never had shoes on before," and he'd let his jaw drop slack, his eyes go vacant, and shamble across the room imitating that hick kid. I didn't find it funny.

When I was in high school, I worked for him part-time in the summers. For a while he was in "women's-better-quality-sportswear" as he used to say, as though it were one word. I moved boxes around. I tried to balance the books. (It was hopeless by then.) And I hated it. I was cut out, so I thought, for something better than helping out the old man. One day I came in wrapped in my usual wretched adolescent surliness that I reserved for the adult world; later—after he'd stepped out for his late-afternoon quick one—Miss Crawford (the fading spinster lady who worked for him right up to the end, even when she was working for promises and he was drunk all the time) told me, "John, it wouldn't hurt you to speak to your father when you come in. You really hurt his feelings, you know."

I was amazed. It had never occurred to me that I could hurt his feelings.

May, 1960

GREEN NIGHTS. Saturday to be exact, at loose ends, driving my father's car up Raysburg Hill not sure where. Lyle was out with Shirley, and Linda was grounded for the weekend. Windows down, rock 'n roll pounding on the radio, so hot in the Valley already I wouldn't need a jacket even if I stayed out all night. That morning, I'd been standing on the porch looking at the dirty Ohio River when my father had uncharacteristically joined me, still in his bathrobe, coffee cup in his hand, and we'd stood there side by side in the swelling heat. He'd smelled like Vitalis. Finally he'd said, "Well, John, it's all over but the shouting." That moment stuck in my mind and bothered me, but I didn't know why.

Beautifully soaring night, but I had nobody to share it with, felt sour and restless. I turned into the parking lot at the Oval. Eighteen, draft card in my pocket as a pass to any bar in town, I pushed through the door.

"What say, gentlemen." Five or six fellow seniors from the Academy were sitting around one of the big circular tables, gallon pitcher of beer in the center.

"Hey Dupre, where are you going to flunk out?"

"Shit, figured I'd flunk out of WVU. How about you?" I sat down and waved at the waitress for a glass.

"Oh, I figure W & J's good enough for me to flunk out of."

"Some sweet meeting," I said. Captain Barkley, our English teacher known as "the Toad," had called us together after school to roast us for slacking off. Now Revington, from the corner where he sat, his long body sprawled bonelessly over the chair, feet on the table, imitated the Toad's voice perfectly: "With the attitude displayed by this class, you gentlemen are going to flunk out of every school foolish enough to admit you. Do I make myself clear?"

I looked around at the laughing faces: the out-the-pike boys, scions of Raysburg money—I could add them up like a handful of dollars—Benton, Clark, and Revington, all Raysburg Steel; Ramsey of the department store, Stewart of the bank, Greer and Phillips of the law firm, Jim Howell, the son of the mayor. I could slip in and out of that crowd easily enough by now, but I never felt comfortable in it.

I saw Revington's dark eyes on mine. "Let's get out of here," he whispered to me out of the side of his mouth.

"See you guys at Raysburg College," I said to them, leaving. That's where the Toad had told us we'd all end up.

Crunching across the gravel of the parking lot, Revington said, "It's no joke, John." He leaned against his father's Porsche and stared up into the sky blanked out with Raysburg's perpetual industrial haze. "This fucking two-bit town," he said, "with its two-bit ambitions."

"Hey," I said, "congratulations." He'd been admitted to Yale. I still had mixed feelings about that. My grades were far better than his, and I might have gone to Yale too, or to any of the Ivy League colleges. In fact, Colonel Sloan had called me into his office to give me hell for not applying to any of them, to which I'd replied, "My father doesn't make that kind of money." True enough, but that was only an excuse, and I still don't know exactly why I chose the state university down at Morgantown. I do remember that after four years at the Academy I wanted to go to school with girls, but there was something more going on. Riding a university education into the upper middle class was the last thing on my mind. I wanted to be a writer, a poet, a folk singer; as Lyle and I kept telling each other, I wanted to *experience life*. I probably chose WVU because that's where I thought *the real people* went.

"You don't suppose the fact that my father went to Yale has anything to do with my getting in, do you?" Revington said in his bitterest voice, scowled, and dragged on his cigarette. It was only recently I'd begun to realize that he wasn't merely another jack-off rich kid.

"Let's go somewhere," I said, meaning Polack Town.

"Yeah," he said without enthusiasm, but then looked quickly at me, grinning. "Hey, I know. Let's go visit the doctor."

"Who's that? What doctor?"

"Don't worry, ace, you'll see."

I followed along behind the Porsche's taillights thinking this must be another one of Revington's mysterious practical jokes. So what did he have planned for me this time? (But it wasn't until later that I realized the full implication of it: he'd also been the one who'd hauled me to that party where I'd met Linda.) He took me to meet, surprisingly, someone our fathers' age, a bandy-legged balding little man with a pipe and a pot belly—Doctor Markapolous.

"Evening, Doctor," Revington said. "This is my friend, John Dupre."

The man half-rose from his chair, grabbed my hand with a grip as solid as a coach's. He had a blunt stubborn bulldog face and bright friendly eyes; I liked him at once. "That's Zoë, my youngest," he said, jerking his head toward the couch where a little pigtailed girl of nine or ten was intently clipping pictures out of a magazine and didn't bother to look up. "You boys want a beer?" Revington and I exchanged significant glances.

He brought in a quart, we drank it in five minutes flat, and he went back for another one. This guy's all right, I thought, although I was perched smugly atop my assessment of the situation. Revington and his father were not exactly close (his standard one-liner: "My father spoke to me once . . . Nineteen fifty-one, I think. Or maybe fifty-two,") and I was thinking: Oh, so here's William's father substitute. But we guzzled down the beer and found ourselves in the middle of a fiery conversation, and, by God, it was just as exciting as any symposium with the boys in the bar. The doctor was down on the rat race as much as we were; we all seemed to be keen on changing the world, "through art," I said. "No," Doctor Markapolous said, "through education. People listen when I talk because I've got that MD after my name, and damn it, it *does* mean something. Learn as much as you can, boys. Never stop learning." And it didn't appear that we were ever going to stop drinking either. He seemed delighted that we'd dropped in; smoking his pipe, yelling, trotting off for more beer, he showed no signs of running down. I'd never met an adult like that before in my life, and eventually I realized that I'd fallen under his spell just as much as Revington must have. I thought: Christ, why couldn't *my* father be like this?

That's when it happened, with me half drunk and fully

relaxed, not expecting to get sucker punched. I saw, out of the corner of my eye, that someone had whisked in and out of the room, an eerily brief flicker like a shy animal coming to look and then gone again before anyone could notice. "Cassandra," the doctor yelled. A girl bounded back into the living room. She was at that difficult age when it's impossible to tell if she's old enough: narrow hips, tiny breasts, the lithe long legs of a colt, but her hair was set, up on rollers as big as orange juice cans, and her legs were shaved. She was barefoot, in minimal camp shorts and a plain white blouse.

"This is my eldest," the doctor said. "Cassandra. This is John Dupre," with a wink to me. "He's a pretty bright kid." I would have expected almost any girl to smile. She did not smile. Not a hint, not a suggestion, not a trace of a smile. She stopped perfectly still, feet flat on the carpet. She had gray eyes—clear, somber, and direct.

Not even summer yet, and she was tanned evenly all over, or maybe it was her Greek blood and the light in the living room, but she looked nearly as dark as mahogany, her complexion Mediterranean, just a shade lighter than olive. A strong face—I don't mean thick or heavy—but a high forehead, positive nose, vigorous unplucked brows, firm lips as beautifully cut as those on one of the exquisite boy athletes the classical Greek sculptors all seemed to have been in love with. Her eyes were widely spaced and almond-shaped, angling upward at the outer margins. When she spoke, her voice was as somber and self-possessed as her eyes: "Hello, John Dupre."

"Come back again," Doctor Markapolous said at one in the morning when Revington and I stumbled up, dead drunk, to leave. I knew I would.

I DON'T suppose I'd seen Cassandra longer than two minutes, but I couldn't sleep that night. I stood leaning on the porch railing staring out at the lights of town reflected in the river. What the hell was the matter with me? I was in love with Linda, wasn't I? So what was I doing getting struck down at first sight like some pathetic Romeo by a little kid just at the edge of puberty? Without having been, I hoped, too obvious about it, I'd extracted her age from her father. Fourteen.

Linda had been fourteen when I'd met her. And there was something else; I'd known it, of course, as an emotional background blur in my mind, but this was the first time I'd been able to put it into words: *I like young girls.* Not children, but girls right at the edge, just as they're beginning to turn into women. But when I'd met Linda, I'd been sixteen; now I was eighteen, and those two extra years felt like a barrier wide as a moat. Where did it come from, what could it possibly mean?

I didn't enjoy thinking about my childhood. Remembering it filled me with painful, skin-crawling embarrassment, but now I seemed to be stuck thinking about it. When I'd been little, I hadn't known any men, and the few I'd met had scared me to death. I couldn't remember much of anything about being four, but that's the year my father had come home from the war, and I gather that I kept telling my mother I wanted *that man* to go away again. By the time I entered grade school, I knew he didn't like me very much, and that was just fine; I didn't like him either. I'd never seen a naked human body other than my own, and I thought that the only difference between boys and girls was the length of their hair. I can remember—I must have been in the first grade—telling my mother that I didn't want to be a boy anymore, that I'd decided to be a girl. I thought it was that simple. She said I couldn't really do that—because "boys and girls have different bodies." That didn't make the least bit of sense to me. I looked at my hand, and it didn't look any different from a girl's hand.

At Jefferson Elementary School on Raysburg Island at the end of the forties, it was obvious that it was much better to be a girl than a boy. At any rate, it was obvious to me. Girls were smarter than boys. Girls *talked* to each other (in fact, some of them never shut up). Girls got to wear pretty clothes. Girls liked doing all the things I liked doing— coloring, reading, sewing, stringing beads, cutting pretty pictures out of magazines. Girls, most of them, were nice to me. But boys weren't nice. They knocked each other down, punched and kicked each other, played dumb boring games like softball. I couldn't imagine why anybody would want to be a boy. I kept pestering my mother to buy me a skirt. Boys in Scotland wear kilts, I said, and I was part Scottish, wasn't I? The skirt she bought me (I picked it out) was a short pleated Stewart tartan that didn't look even remotely like a kilt. I wore it every day after school. "Don't you ever let your father catch you like that," my mother told me.

I was a solitary kid, but I did have a few friends, and they were always girls. Sometimes we played dress-up, and I tried on their clothes every chance I got. Halloween was my favorite holiday, the one day a year I could wear anything I wanted; until I grew old enough to know better, I used the occasion to turn myself into a series of storybook princesses. The second grade sticks in my mind as the prettiest costume I ever wore, the only time I was ever photographed dressed as a girl. I had decided to be Alice in Wonderland. I knew what Alice looked like because I had books about her, and I insisted that I wanted to look like her all the way down to the finest detail. I don't know how my mother managed to assemble the costume—maybe she rented it somewhere— but she found the right blond wig, the right dress and apron, and even the right frothy petticoat to make the skirt flare. I borrowed patent leather shoes from one of my girlfriends. When I showed up at school, the other kids teased me briefly and then, strangely enough, *stopped* teasing me. It's almost as though they forgot I was a boy—or maybe I simply seemed more natural to them as a girl. By the end of the day, the other girls were calling me Alice as though it was really my name. I wanted Halloween to last forever.

I couldn't feel any anger toward my mother for aiding and abetting me. Her indifference still felt like kindness. "He'll outgrow it," I overheard her saying to my father. And she'd been right; I had outgrown it—if burying it in myself and escaping into a compulsive world of fantasy and science fiction was outgrowing it. When I'd been little, I'd been oddly proud of my girlishness, but gradually I'd learned to be ashamed of it. By the time I was twelve, I never would have admitted to anyone that I still sometimes wanted to be a girl. I hated it when the kids at Jefferson called me "Miss Dupre." A boy who wanted to be a girl was a *sissy*, and that was the most shameful disgusting thing a boy could be. I learned to be careful.

I paced up and down on the porch, cutting into memory, trying to make sense of all this. The second grade, I remembered, was also the year I fell in love with a girl in my class named Nancy Clark. Her mother set her blond hair into perfect Shirley Temple sausage curls and sent her to school every day in party dresses and classic Mary Janes, and I thought Nancy was so wonderful that I couldn't imagine why everyone in the world wasn't in love with her. She even tap danced; I remember admiring her in school recitals. Nancy was— I was about to say "shy," but that's not right. She was the kind of girl who, when she wanted to tell you something, bent close and whispered in your ear. And she liked me as much as I liked her. We walked around the school yard holding hands, sat together when we could, and announced to the world that we were going to get married. I was delighted to be her boyfriend, and I fully intended to marry her—and I wanted to be just like her. At the time, those things did not seem contradictory.

Seven-year-old boys at Jefferson Elementary did not have girlfriends. A normal boy—a *real* boy—would have rather died on the rack than be seen walking around at recess holding hands with a girl. So Nancy and I must have made quite a spectacle of ourselves, and I think now that there must have been some adult plot to separate us. In the third grade, we were put into different classes. We got older and drifted apart. I've forgotten everyone else at Jefferson, but I'll never forget Nancy Clark.

I WAS still pacing when dawn began to whiten the streets. My mind kept coming back to Linda and Cassandra. Then, as suddenly as slicing through a knot, I found something more. *Fourteen,* the magic age, had been another bad year for me, another year I'd been doing my best to forget. Halfway through the eighth grade, I'd begun to sprout a blond fuzz of pubic hair. One morning I woke out of my first wet dream; I'd read enough to know what it meant, so I'd been expecting it, but still my reaction was violent. I shut myself in the bathroom and threw up. I remember thinking: *It's true. I really am a boy. There's no escape from it.* And then I tried to escape from it.

I could not possibly have worked up the courage to walk up to a newsstand and buy a copy of *Seventeen,* but it was easy enough to read it in the library—hiding it inside another magazine. *Seventeen* told you, in as much detail as you'd ever want or need, exactly how to be a girl. I read it, and other girls' magazines, cover to cover, storing information I could never use. I knew, in theory at least, how to set hair, how to put on makeup, what styles were in and what were out. At home I swiped the Sears Roebuck catalogue, clipped pictures out of the girls' section, and pasted them into a secret scrapbook. I could get lost for hours in that scrapbook. I had compelling, intense, and vividly detailed fantasies. They weren't sexual fantasies. I never imagined a sexual act of any kind with anybody, and it never occurred to me to play with myself. I imagined ordinary everyday events like setting my hair and shaving my legs, putting on a nice outfit—nothing sexy, just the normal clothes a fourteen-year-old girl would wear, a blouse and a skirt, bobby socks and loafers—and walking over to town to meet my girlfriends and go to a matinee at the Liberty. Back in the real world, summer twilight drove me crazy, filled me with an unbearable anguish that felt like an iron ring crushing my lungs and stomach; all I could find to do for it was ride my bike around and around the Island until darkness brought the illusion of relief.

I decided that I should match the weight-height charts for teenage girls. Those dopey charts were everywhere in those days; the one I'd found was for "ideal" weight and was broken down not only by height but also by age and "frame." I already fit into the section for fourteen-year-old girls of my height with a "heavy frame," but that wasn't good enough for me. The top end of the "light frame" range was 112, the bottom end 98, and I became obsessed with those numbers. I went on cottage cheese and grapefruit diets until I weighed 110. I found a million excuses not to visit the barber shop, feathered my hair over my forehead to look like bangs, dressed to the teeth in pink and charcoal—the colors that were in that year—and painted my nails with clear polish. When my father was deeply displeased with me, he always expressed himself through my mother. "Your father is very upset," she said.

"But he does it!" I said. My mother explained to me that there was a difference between a grown-up businessman getting a manicure once a month and a fourteen-year-old boy wearing nail polish. And, while she was on the subject of my appearance, she really had to mention my hair. It was a disgrace, and if I didn't do something about it, my father certainly would.

I stopped wearing nail polish, got a haircut, and decided to try for the low end of the weight chart. "You're not going on any more crazy diets," my mother said. "You're thin enough already." So I got sneaky—found ways to miss meals, rearrange things on my plate so it looked as though I'd been eating, secretly dump food into the garbage. My mother took me to our family doctor. I told him three lies: that I felt fine, always ate as much as I wanted, and was never hungry. Breaking 100 pounds was one of the hardest things I'd ever done in my life, and I was enormously pleased with myself. For a few days, I even weighed 98. Then it occurred to me that if I could get my weight below 98, I'd be even *better* than a real girl. But that fall my father sent me to the Raysburg Military Academy, and all of a sudden I had more serious things to worry about than trying to drop off the bottom of a girls' weight chart.

I'd put all that—my miserable embarrassing childhood—

behind me, or so I'd thought. I was eighteen now, and I was doing just fine. Nobody any longer suspected that there was anything wrong with me. Finding Linda had made everything fall into place, and up until tonight, that had been enough. So what had happened to me in those two minutes I'd seen Cassandra Markapolous? By then I'd read not only Freud and Havelock Ellis but every book on sex in the library. I'd learned what "fetishes" were and knew that I had quite a few of them myself; I adored anything that struck me as archetypically feminine: high heels, stockings and petticoats, lipstick and nail polish, little white gloves, a majorette's short skirt and white boots. According to everything I'd read, with a childhood like mine, I might well have been a homosexual, but I knew that I wasn't. My friendship with Lyle was the most intense I'd ever had with anybody, but I didn't want to go to bed with him; not only was the thought of it repellent, it was *utterly ridiculous*. And I did want to go to bed with Linda—sometime, in the dim future. But suddenly there'd been this little kid, Cassandra, too young for me, breastless, tanned, with her direct tomboy gaze and her hair up in rollers—a boy-girl—which is what, in the privacy of my mind, in my bed, in the dark, I still felt myself to be. All of the books I'd read hadn't helped a bit. Not a single one of them had described anyone who sounded the least bit like me. It was full daylight, and I was still immensely confused.

GREEN MORNINGS. I can't stay confused for long: life's too sweet. Only a few months ago, I'd hated the sound

alarm tearing away my sleep, had awakened into the
darkness thinking: oh Christ, not another day! My senior had been an enormous ordeal to get through, like
prison or Marine boot camp, but now the Boards are over,
classes are over, I'm going away to university in the fall, and
I have Linda. The green wind blowing in is hot already. I'm
awake ahead of the alarm, and by noon the sun will be burning bright. I slip out of bed, feel the good ache of use in my
legs, the sweat under my arms. I slip into jock, shorts, and
sneakers and bicycle down to the Island stadium. Saturday
morning and nobody up yet, the track deserted except for
me and the birds, I run two miles at just under fourteen minutes. It seems slow to me, a romp; I'm not pushing myself in
the least. Drifting home to the click of the wheels, I'm astonished again at my own happiness and good fortune. It's so
big and fat and sunny I can never quite get ahold of it: life
broad and straight as Front Street and I can't possibly lose.

But in an hour I'm wondering how the hell I'm going to
get through the rest of the day. It takes me only ten minutes
to get sick of playing the guitar. Now I'm as tense and twanging as my steel strings. I pick the car keys off the dining room
table. It's only a short drive to Cassandra's house. I've seen a lot
of her father lately but next to nothing of her. I'm beginning
to suspect that she's avoiding me. I arrive around noon. The
doctor, as I know damned well, is on the golf course. The first
person I see is little Zoë. She's playing all alone, riding her
bicycle from one end of the street to the other. "My daddy's
not home," she says whizzing by me. I sit down on the glider.

"Do you know when he'll be back?"

"I don't know," she yells on the next pass.

A glimpse of Cassandra just inside the front door—babydoll pajamas, hammer blow to my ribs. She doesn't come out onto the porch. "Dad's not home."

"That's what your sister said."

"I think he's playing golf or something." She's gone. I wait. It's turning into a viciously hot day.

In a few minutes Cassandra returns in shorts and a halter top, throws herself down on the glider next to me but doesn't look in my direction at all. She has a wonderful thick mane of reddish-brown hair. She puts her feet up on the railing; the soles are filthy. (Does she ever were shoes?) Her knees are knobby and the bones in her ankles sharp as cherry stones. "I don't know when he'll be back," she says. (Does she ever smile?) We swing gently in the glider. (Does she ever talk?)

My mouth's gone dry, and I can actually feel the increase in my heart rate. I'm just on the point of standing up to leave when Zoë parks her bike, runs up the steps, and, without any warning at all, jumps smack onto my lap. It's as though Cassandra got all the Greek blood and there wasn't any left for her sister; Zoë's got a cute pink-cheeked oval face, a perfect little cupid's bow mouth, and huge long-lashed eyes, blue as cornflowers. She's almost too pretty, like a sentimentalized painting of a cherub. And now what am I supposed to do with her sitting on me—pet her like a cat? And isn't she a little big for this sort of thing?

"Zoë," Cassandra says, her voice sharp, "don't be a pest."

"I'm not a pest. Ask John. Am I a pest?"

"Zo-*ë!*" Cassandra's voice has a distinct warning in it.

Little sister gives big sister a murderous look, slips off my lap, and marches into the house, banging the door behind her. "Good grief," Cassandra says, lets her head fall back so she's looking directly up at the ceiling.

"Well, tell your dad I was here, will you?" But I continue to sit there.

Still without looking at me, she says, "You go with Linda Edmonds, don't you?"

"Yes. How did you know that?"

"Oh, I heard it."

"How about you? Do you go with anybody?"

"Oh sure. They line up halfway around the block." What's that supposed to be, a joke? She'd said it with no expression in her voice at all.

Suddenly I can't stand to be there any longer. I'm on my feet with sweat pouring down my sides, hear myself saying again, asininely, "Tell your dad I was here."

She doesn't answer, and I'm in the car and gone. I'm making a fool of myself; that much is obvious. Stop thinking about Cassandra Markapolous, I tell myself. She's too young for you. And besides, you're in love with Linda.

YEAH, IT really did seem that Linda and I were in love. As I squired her through all of our year-end functions, the dances and the Prom and the graduation parties and banquets, I'd never been happier with a girl or felt better about myself as a male; going steady or not, she was "my girl," and everyone knew it. She might have been something of an embarrassment when I'd started dating her, but she wasn't any longer. If I'd wanted a girl to show off, she'd grown into the role perfectly. I remember one night, a dinner party, the dining room table set with white linen and candles, aureoles of soft light on the crystal, flames glinting from the silver, and Linda stepping into the scene as though she'd prepared particularly for candlelight and white linen—a short powder-blue cocktail dress and exquisite white heels to show off her legs, her schoolgirl pageboy replaced by a stylish bouffant, her nails polished and as lucent as the silverware—graceful and charming, outshining the table. Or Linda at the Prom in a formal gown, floating on the dance floor with a rustle of crinolines, as easy to lead as thistledown, avatar of a Southern belle.

But something was going wrong so subtly that I couldn't quite put my finger on it. Although they'd been invited to my graduation, her parents didn't come. At the time, I didn't think a thing of it. And there I was, the Salutatorian, standing up in front of the lectern, reading my speech to my friends and classmates, my teachers, to everybody in the whole goddamned Academy. I glanced at Linda only once. She was sitting with my parents, looking up at me with her huge eyes and beautiful smile. To keep my panic under control, I stared hard at the paper in front of me. My voice, like that of a distant Doppelgänger, was reverberating out of the PA speakers. "We can make ourselves in any image we desire," I was saying. "We are not merely creatures of environment to

103

be measured and tabulated by the social sciences, but, if we control habit instead of habit controlling us, we are masters of our fate. As Will James writes: 'Keep the faculty of effort alive in you by a little gratuitous exercise every day. That is, be systematically ascetic or heroic in little unnecessary points, do every day or two something for no other reason than you would rather not do it, so that when the hour of dire need draws nigh, it may find you not unnerved and untrained to stand the test.'"

Then it was over, high school was over. Lyle pumped my hand. "Wonderful speech, boy. You really told them." My father congratulated me, my mother was crying, and I couldn't stand it, had to be alone for a minute with Linda. I walked her away from the crowd to a tree, took her white-gloved hands in mine. Suddenly the full weight of it sunk into me for the first time; it wasn't a game, not a story I was writing or a play I was starring in. I wasn't in high school anymore, and now I'd have to leave. Jesus, I thought, I can't let her see me cry. She threw her arms around me and hung on.

"It's all right, John," she said, "It's all right. It's all right."

The last event of the year was final drills. I'd been looking forward to it, but our parade was rained out.

June, 1960

AS SOON as my graduation festivities were over, Linda's parents whisked her away to Greenbrier Springs, and I was left feeling deflated. What was I supposed to do with the three empty months before I went away to college? I didn't seem capable of even getting through the two weeks Linda was going to be out of town. I'd never had sexual dreams about girls I actually knew, but now I began to dream of Linda every night, and the dreams were potently sexual. In each of them we'd be surrounded by people, she'd be dressed beautifully and I'd want her, we'd go off to be alone, begin to make out, but just at the moment when something began to happen, I'd wake up. They weren't wet dreams; I was always barely short of coming when my eyes would pop open and I'd find myself alone in my bed in the sticky West Virginia heat, usually just at dawn. I still had vestigial guilt feelings about jerking off—not that it was morally wrong, but that it was somehow unmanly—so tried not to, but lost the battle a few times. After seven successive nights, the dreams stopped.

Lyle had an old Polish grandmother who knew about dreams, so he professed to know about them too. "It means something," he said with a smug nod like Merlin breaking in a new apprentice.

"Yeah, but what?"

"Maybe it means it's the real thing." I thought so too, but I didn't know what to do with it.

One night in the Pines, at four in the morning and so plastered I could scarcely sit upright, it came to me in a flash of beery revelation: I should tell her that I loved her. Now I can't imagine how I thought that would solve anything, but

I did. The actual words—*I love you*—were very important then, practically a magical formula, and neither of us had ever spoken them.

I remember that I didn't mean either "marry me" or "sleep with me." The first was impossible—sixteen-year-olds didn't marry eighteen-year-olds unless they were hillbilly kids from downstate; and the second was just as impossible—you didn't have sex with nice girls, and Linda was nothing if not a nice girl. My feelings were powerful and my thoughts were vague, so trying now to guess what it is that I wanted from her is a work of pure archeology from a site almost devoid of clues—not much more than a broken pot here, a few flints there, and a ruined hearth stone. This is the best I can do: I was about to ride off to battle with the world, off to university and the beginning of my "career" (whatever it might turn out to be), and I wanted her silken sleeve to tie to my helm. Even though I hadn't learned the term yet, no troubadour poet could have been more imbued with the spirit of Courtly Love than I was. I wasn't after her treasure beyond price, the pearl of her virginity, didn't expect her to sit home and pine while I was gone, didn't think that she'd never date another guy. I suppose what I wanted was for her to be "my girl"— there for me at Christmas and summer vacations, a "lodestar to action" as I wrote in my diary. So if I could get her to accept me as her knight, get her to say, "I love you too," I could go galloping off with a clear heart, chop my way to straight A's and graduate with honors—in short, do all the things I was supposed to do, the things that my entire schooling and my parents' expectations had set me up to do, because I'd be doing it *for her.* At the end of the quest: my lady.

But it didn't happen that way. She came back to town near the end of June, and I'd never seen her in such a sour prickly distant mood. She'd had a rotten time, she said, had fought every day with her mother. "I don't know how I'm going to live with her for the next two years. It feels like I'm down in the Moundsville Pen." She told me that she'd changed over the trip; I didn't know what she could possibly mean. Even though she was never going to tan in her life and knew it, she took to hanging our with the tennis crowd at the Raysburg Country Club (no Jews or Polacks, if you please), would sit under a huge umbrella and play hearts with the other rich girls and watch her pal, Sue Eberhardt, bash the ball around. I'd never thought of her as a country-club girl, and it bothered me. Because of a wink from Revington, I was on permanent unofficial guest status there, so, carrying my unspoken "I love you" around like a heavy gold nugget in my mouth, I went to the Club every afternoon. There wasn't a whole hell of a lot for me to do there. I didn't play tennis or golf and wasn't much of a swimmer either. I'd turned eighteen though, so I could get mildly plastered in the desiccating sun. We'd read Fitzgerald in Senior English, and I remember that I sat there on the terrace dizzily identifying with Jay Gatsby. I put all the beers on Revington's tab.

Linda and I danced in the empty ballroom. I'd drop a quarter into the jukebox, play "Unchained Melody" (our song) five times in a row, and hold her as tight as she'd let me. We weren't able to talk easily, and I began to wonder if she'd ever really liked me, began to feel like an unwanted dog, particularly on the nights I tagged along all the way to her house, stayed for dinner, stayed to watch TV, stayed until she threw me out at midnight. She'd still kiss me, but her heart didn't seem to be in it.

There were recurring motifs in the funny papers in the fifties; one of them was of an enormous safe being lowered on block and tackle down the side of a tall building. Just as you know from the very first panel that it's going to, the safe always breaks free to come plummeting down on Donald Duck's unsuspecting head. I kept a diary all that summer, so I know that the night the safe fell on me was a Tuesday.

Linda and I were sitting on the back porch silking corn before dinner. The fashion historian in me noted that she was wearing a dress and, even though it was a hot day, nylons, but the novelist must have been out to lunch because the only dialogue I recorded was—

Linda: "You're just like my mother. You win every argument in the end."

Me: "We're not having an argument. What is there to win?"

Linda: "I don't know, but I just have the feeling that nothing I say is going to matter."

The intervening conversation is lost now, but I remember the appalling heat, the dull ache in my chest, the feel of the corn silk under my fingers, and the trapped panicky sensation of getting nowhere. I wrote down that she said: "I get so sick of everybody picking at me all the time."

At dinner she made a terrible Freudian slip and called me "mother." It was a late dinner, the maid had gone home, and Linda and I did the dishes. From here on I don't need my sketchy diary because it's still, after all these years, as clear in my mind as a movie I can take out and rerun. Her parents are in the TV room; we can hear the sound of the set. Linda is washing, wearing an apron, one of those silly things with the big bow in the back, so full and flounced it's practically a pinafore. I'm drying. I pick up the plates one at a time; as I polish them with the tea towel, I pace up and down the full length of the kitchen.

"Stop that," she says. "You look like an animal in a cage."

"I feel like an animal in a cage."

"What's the matter?" She doesn't sound the least bit sympathetic.

"I have something to say to you."

"Well, say it."

"You don't give me a chance."

"All right. I'll be quiet for ten minutes."

We finish the dishes in a silence that's growing thicker and nastier by the second. She jerks the bow out of her apron, hangs it up, and snaps at me, "I'm going in to watch TV."

"Linda, please come outside a minute."

"All right." We bang through the screen door and walk out across the lawn to the rose bushes.

"What is it, John? What's the matter?"

I'm mute and miserable. We stand there, faced off. Her

father steps through the kitchen door and out onto the back porch. "Here comes your father. I love you."

Charlie Edmonds surveys the night, trims a cigar and lights it. If he sees us standing by the rose bushes—and he'd have to be blind not to—he doesn't let on. He puffs and looks at the stars. He turns and walks back inside. I've been watching her father, and she's been watching me.

She hears the screen door slam and says, "I'm flattered but exasperated."

"What does that mean?"

"I don't love anybody. Not even my parents. Sometimes I think I don't feel anything at all about anybody." I don't know what to say to that. She smiles sadly. "Well, at least it wasn't what I thought you were going to say."

"What did you expect?"

"Scat cat."

"Linda, I could never say that to you."

"No? I suppose I'm glad to hear that."

"Don't you like me at all?"

"Of course I do, silly. I used to be crazy about you."

"What about now?"

She shrugs, and I start to cry. I haven't cried like that since I was a child, not merely moist eyes but all out, bent over and sobbing. I'm astonished; I can't believe it's happening. Linda's holding onto me and saying, "Oh baby! Oh baby, don't."

"I love you more than anything in the world."

"Don't say that, please. Oh damn, I wish I were dead."

It's over quickly, and suddenly we've become impossibly

formal. We take several turns across the lawn, holding hands. I kiss her goodbye and then, without going back into the house, walk straight to my father's car and drive away.

Naturally I went looking for Lyle, found him on the first try, in the Owl, and naturally I got roaring drunk. I didn't tell him about it. We made plans to take a trip the next day, it didn't much matter where. I woke up with a bad hangover, feeling squashed and bleak, but nothing like real pain. Lyle picked me up after lunch and we drove down to Harrod. The little stadium where he had won and I had placed in the mile was open; we walked into it and around the track, around and around the track. The sky, full of postcard puff-ball clouds, was blue as Linda's eyes.

"Well, it's all over, boy. What do you say?"

"Yeah, we made it, didn't we?"

"You going out for cross-country?"

"Yeah, how about you?"

"Of course I am," he said as though I should have known better than to ask. "We've got to keep at it. We've got to keep on training. That's where we're going to find it. You know there's only one thing for us, John."

"What's that?"

"The marathon." He said the word the way other guys might have said "pussy."

Suddenly my spirits went up like a weather balloon and I was absurdly happy. I wasn't in love with her, I thought. It must have been some kind of an illusion. Lyle and I drank our way back to Raysburg, and I got more and more giddy and out of control. By the time he dropped me off at my house, I was a step away from turning into the village idiot. I still hadn't told him about it. I fell asleep at once, woke around dawn. Now I can't improve on the words I wrote in my diary: "It felt as though I had started to bleed inside."

I finally got even with Lyle for all those middle-of-the-night phone calls, woke up his father and then him. He didn't let me down; he was over in twenty minutes. For the next few weeks he tried to console me in damned near every bar in town. He read to me from a Buddhist Sutra: "It is better to live alone; there is no companionship with a fool; let a man walk alone, let him commit no sin, having few wishes, like an elephant in a forest."

Great consolation, Lyle!

July, 1960

"HOW DO you start this damned thing?"

"Just turn the key to the right . . . Listen, Lyle, I know I'm as drunk as hell and I'm having a hard time getting my words . . . my words out right . . . but I feel I've got to say something. Am I making any sense?"

"Yeah, sure. Sure you're making sense. How do we get to the Greek's?"

"You know, keep south. It's on 34th Street . . . Jesus, Lyle, I need a girl. Goddamn it, I'm drunk. What happened to Revington?"

"He took his own car, remember? Daddy's Porsche . . . the asshole."

"Thanks for driving, boy. I couldn't even find the street . . . Jesus, what am I thinking about?" Lyle's so pitiful sometimes when he gets drunk. Am I getting that way? "I feel so lonely sometimes. You've got to listen to me . . . Jesus, I wanted it so much with Linda, and it didn't work out. Goddamn, I'm so fucking drunk." Christ, can hardly stand up, like bailing off that truck rolling through Harrod all juiced; wow, the ground comes up like thunder.

"Whiskey."

"Yeah, sure. A double." Chase it with beer, hits and burns, stomach twists, hate the taste. Revington's got a wad of bills big enough to choke a horse, drinking them down like water. Why the hell can't I drink all night and not get any drunker than he gets?

"Watch the door frame there, John."

"Hey, thanks a hell of a lot, Lyle. Really. I mean it. I may be drunk, but I really mean it . . . Hey, William, can you lend me some money?"

THE FLOOR.

"Why do you guys come in here if you can't hold it?"

Money gone, money gone, ho ho, the money's gone, money gone, all gone, ho ho, the money's gone. "Come on, John, get up."

Bouncing over the railroad tracks, Shirley Pulenski lives down here, the train comes by every hour it seems like, and she was a Modigliani in the yellow lamplight with her glasses off. Lyle was snowed. And later in Papa's, beer and whiskey, beer and whiskey, on the bus, ride jumbles it all up into ecstasy, so great like Buddy Holly's roller coaster, throwing a stone at Lyle's window, and end up at the Greek's. Jesus, the music, Jesus Christ, the music, blasting, pounding, the air is music, the people are music. And Lyle and I were crying somewhere when the waitress came up, said, "What's the matter, boys?" Said to me, "You have a girl, don't you?" "Yeah," I said, I supposed I did. "Well, go to her." But not as simple as that. Linda.

"Here. Don't spill it."

"Hey, thanks a hell of a lot. I really mean it."

Jukebox, laughter, through a wall of cotton, booth is a boat on wings. Flame of a match lights Revington's dark face, flows and blurs and is gone. Outside it's raining. Single deep drag, clearly but terribly distant, sound of burning cigarette, crackle, then he's pounding on the chair with his fists, jumps up to dance with some girl.

"Lyle, listen . . . am I talking all right? Jesus . . . listen. She doesn't know. She doesn't care. She hasn't got any feelings. If I could see her cry just once, it'd break the spell, but I never will. I'll cry over her, but she'll never cry over me . . . Jesus, she's more of an adult than I am over the whole thing . . . Jesus fuck, Lyle, it's hard trying to be a man."

"Yeah, I know."

"Jesus, Lyle, it's over. We're all going to leave. It'll never be the same again."

Linda. The way she'd practically get in my clothes with

me. Here we are with the crappy back stairs, the pisshouse painted pink, the cigars, the Greek music. And what am I doing here? I'm more of a girl than Linda is. "Send it back to the old country," the fat man says, but what does he know? And can't they all hear it, that soft roaring? What is it? Jesus, sliding down. "Hey boy, sit up. Come on."

Rain, sweeping water, torrents down neon streets, pounding onto cars, spilling into gutters, overflowing. Lightning, sudden, CRACK. Greece, that wailing music says: rise up, rise up! Cassandra, heart in my throat when I see her. Boy-girl. Somewhere a pulse, a throb. Wish I could talk or something. Linda wanted a real boy. Alone always, no real contact ever, nothing done and nothing ever will. "Jesus, he's a mess. Give me a hand, will you?"

In bed? How the fuck did I get in bed? I loved her, I love her, dumb words, repeat them forever. When I drink, when I drink. Jesus, I knew somewhere like I did. He could never even get, girl in he got. Jesus, Linda in the heat. Can hardly and whiskey. Jumbling in alcohol, so great on the jukebox, and not get any drunker than he gets? Revington pounding on the chairs. Hey, can you lend me some money? Never saw Linda's bedroom, never will. Could I kiss Cassandra, just a child? Lyle, you and your crying drunks are so close to me now. Greeks, how many times the whiskey gets to you, thanks one hell of a lot, boy, I really mean it, half an hour apart like a goddamned thing at least. Death coming at any rate and nothing's done. Blasting affected and I can't see glowing that she's practically day as to you.

EVEN THOUGH I threw up half a dozen times during the night, neither of my parents said a word to me about it when I crawled out of bed around eleven. To prove to myself that I was still alive, I walked down to the stadium. My joints seemed to be full of sand and ground glass. I jogged a slow head-pounding two miles, came home and took a shower with the water on full cold. Then I managed to get an eggnog into myself, sat on the bank and tossed pebbles into the river. The day was unbearably hot. Sweat it out, you asshole, I told myself. By late afternoon the pain had receded enough, and I went home and asked my father for the car. He gave me the keys with a wink. "You're only eighteen once," he said. It didn't mean a thing to me then.

I found Cassandra lying in her backyard on a beach towel. She was wearing a bikini that didn't leave a whole hell of a lot to the imagination; I was stopped by some nameless dread, stared at her. She had a figure that made Linda's look voluptuous. I mean Linda was slender and small-breasted, but Cassandra— Well, lying on her back, she didn't appear to need the top of her swimsuit any more than I would have; her hips were narrow, her legs long and knobby, her stomach flat and hard. She was all straight lines and sharp angles, could have been a tall tough eleven as easily as fourteen. She looked much the way I had wanted to when *I'd* been fourteen (and that was something I would have preferred not to remember). Feeling both excited and obscurely guilty, I threw myself down on the grass next to her. She didn't open her eyes, but I knew that she must have heard me coming. "Hi, Cassandra," I said.

"Hello, John," she said, her eyes still shut. I heard a tickle in her voice as though she was making fun of me. She was tanned as brown as a buckeye.

"Look," I said, "I think your father's a great guy, but . . . Well, sometimes I'd like to come over here to see *you*." It was a speech I'd written, edited, polished, and rehearsed all morning.

She sat up and looked at me with those gray, grave, unsmiling eyes. I didn't have the remotest idea what she was thinking. Then she said, "Do you want to stay for dinner?"

"Sure."

She put on her sunglasses, vanished behind the blank green mirrors of them, left me without the hope of a clue. "Well," she said slowly, "you must not go for the Marilyn Monroe type." She turned out to be frighteningly bright, and she'd read Jack Kerouac too.

On the pretext of going to the corner store, we walked along the river bank at twilight. I tried to hold her hand, and she said, "I'm not the hand-holding type, John Dupre," but our mouths came together easily, without any fuss— with a fierceness I'd never known before. She had none of Linda's coyness or elusiveness, just intent, single-minded lips and teeth and tongue and clinging until we were both panting and she said, "Doggone it, John, I feel like flopping over on my back for you right here and now," which scared me half to death. As we walked back to her house, still not holding hands, she said, "Watch out for Zoë. She's a little spy." It never occurred to either of us that her parents might not object to her seeing me.

It *was* her little sister, of course, who spilled the beans. Doctor Markapolous took me aside and said, in a voice so severe that it took me a while to realize that he was kidding me, "My youngest tells me that you have been taking liberties with my eldest." I didn't know what to say. "Look, John, cut the cloak and dagger business, will you? I don't care if you want to see Cassandra. She's old enough to take care of herself." It was out in the open after that, and I saw Cassy nearly every day until I left for Morgantown in the fall.

One Saturday morning I turned up and found her in the house alone. "Dad's golfing. Mom and Zoë are shopping." She was wearing her standard summer uniform: shorts and blouse, bare feet. She must have set her wonderful burnt sienna hair the night before; it was tumbling around her shoulders in thick fat curls. "When Mom and Zoë go shopping," she said, "they're always gone all day." It was as though we were both in a trance. I felt light-headed, detached, nearly depersonalized. She closed the front door and locked it. I followed her upstairs.

Her bedroom was a surprise; except for the filmy white drapes, it wasn't so very different from mine: a casual clutter, lots of books. I don't know what I'd expected, leftover childhood dolls perhaps (she told me later she'd never played with dolls), but the only overt signs of femininity were a pile of plain cotton underwear thrown into a corner and a single pair of nylons draped over the arm of a chair.

Of course it never occurred to either of us to take our clothes off; I kicked off my sneakers, and we stretched out on her bed. When I gradually began to realize that we had enough time, that she wasn't going anywhere, that she wasn't going to stop me, I was nearly overwhelmed.

Among the many things I never would have told my closest friends, no matter how drunkenly confessional we might get at one in the morning, was that girls' breasts didn't have the dominating fascination for me that they seemed to have for every other male I knew, and now, with Cassandra, it wasn't just that her boyish figure didn't bother me—I was stunned by the beauty of it. I couldn't imagine anything more perfect than her long-legged coltish adolescent body, anything more beautiful than her concentrated Athena-gray eyes and face as strong as a hawk's. And then, with our mouths screwed tight together, our legs intertwined, the impossible began to happen: all of me, from my toes to my eyeballs, seemed to be draining to a single point. A moment of steel panic—something about not wanting to embarrass her and another fear even more obscure, that I might mysteriously rip myself apart—but I passed through it, broke into absolute loveliness.

I drifted back to a great astonishment. Linda Edmonds? Who the hell was Linda Edmonds? "Hey," I said, "do you think we should go downstairs?" The house was very quiet.

"Did you have an orgasm?" she said.

I wasn't shocked so much as totally disoriented. "Yeah," I said. "Yeah, I did."

"Is it all wet?"

I had to laugh at that. "Of course it's all wet. What do you think?"

"I don't know. Good grief, do you think I do this all the time?" Very lightly, she touched me between the legs. "Does it feel icky?"

What was happening now was so strange that I couldn't possibly laugh. Her eyes were serious and questioning. "No, it's wonderful. It's great."

"I can't imagine what it must be like . . . Did it hurt? . . . I mean the way we're built, it's designed to be inside me."

"No, it didn't hurt."

"This has never happened to me before."

"It's never happened to me before either."

"You're kidding me."

"No, I'm not."

"Not with Linda Edmonds?"

"No, never." Her face was changing. "Cassandra," I said, "you look like the cat that ate the canary."

"Well, you look kind of smug yourself, John Dupre . . . Come on, maybe we'd better go back downstairs. If they caught us, it'd be horrible."

It seems ridiculous, the details that I remember after all these years: I hadn't had much of an appetite since Linda and I had split up, but now I was enormously hungry, ate two bologna sandwiches with Velveeta cheese and sweet pickles.

August, 1960

"WHAT PARTY? Whose party?"

"Sue Eberhardt's."

"Who's going to be there?"

"That crowd of Canden High girls in her class . . . you know."

Cassandra sank onto the couch as suddenly as if she'd been kicked behind the knees. "Good grief," she said, "the big kids."

"They're not that big."

"Aren't you supposed to call a girl up ahead of time and give her some warning? Isn't that how it's supposed to be done?"

"I didn't have any warning . . . She doesn't expect me to come, just invited me out of politeness. If you really want somebody at your party, you don't ask them the day it's happening, but she probably started feeling guilty at the last minute and thought, well, I'd better invite John for old times' sake . . . So here I am invited. So I can bring somebody. So I'm going to bring you."

"Doggone it, now I wish I'd taken a bath today. I look like holy hell."

"You could never look like holy hell, Cassy."

"Yeah, I do. My hair's all ratty . . . What am I going to wear?"

"Wear your new white skirt," Zoë said from the other side of the room.

"Shut up, Zo . . . How do those girls dress?"

"To the teeth."

"That's what I thought . . . John, are you sure you want to take me?"

"Perfectly sure."

She stood and walked upstairs. When she came back five minutes later, she'd changed into jeans and a boy's shirt, had brushed her hair. She'd been right: it did need a washing: straight and shiny with oil.

"You aren't going to a party dressed like that, are you?" Zoë said. "Mom would have a fit."

"Zoë, dear, how's Mom going to know unless you tell her?"

Zoë looked at her sister like a wide-eyed angel. "Oh, I wouldn't do that." (But she did.)

In the car, Cassandra said, "You know, John, you can't win. If you're different, they pick you to pieces, but if you try to be like them, that doesn't work either because they know you don't mean it."

"So to hell with them."

"That's easy enough for you to say. You're not a girl."

She sat stiffly, her arms wrapped around herself. "You know, I've had my period for over a year now, and I'm beginning to get the horrible feeling that these are the only tits I'm ever going to get."

I was shocked. I couldn't get used to her. Girls just didn't say things like that. "It doesn't matter," I told her.

"Maybe it doesn't matter to you . . . but you're going

away to college, and I don't want to spend every Saturday night at home alone."

"You won't. You're going to have boyfriends, Cassy. You're going to have lots of them."

"I wish I believed it."

"Well, believe me, then. I'm male and I should know. It's like that joke you made before I knew you well enough to know it was a joke . . . but it's going to be true. They *are* going to be lined up halfway around the block."

All those damned Canden High kids were driving their daddies' expensive cars, and I had to park a block away from the house. I didn't bother to lock the old blue Dodge, grabbed my guitar out of the back, took Cassandra by the hand and led her up the sidewalk under the stately green trees. For once she didn't say, "I'm not the hand-holding type, John Dupre," but instead gave me that gloomy, contracted look and said again, "The big kids."

"Oh, for Christ's sake. Some of those girls aren't more than a year older than you are."

I rang the bell, stood waiting for the door to open. There's no excuse for these people to have so much money, I was thinking, to have such exquisitely perfumed and pampered and petted and delectable daughters. Then, with an unpleasant twist of *déjà vu,* I remembered that I'd met Linda at a party exactly like this one. The door swung inward, and there was Miss Susan Eberhardt in a sleeveless white dress. Her bare shoulders, browned at the country club, shone like satin. She looked at me, she looked at Cassandra, and then she looked at me again. I've got to give her credit: she didn't lose her smile. "How nice to see you, John. Hello, Cassy, what a surprise."

Of course Revington was there. I was holding hands with Cassandra, and he sent me a look so loaded it was in danger of capsizing; his eyebrows were shoved halfway up his forehead.

"William," she said to him in a small sour voice.

"Miss Markapolous," he murmured, and then with an avuncular gallantry gathered her up under one arm and began introducing her around the room. His eyes said to me: "We'll talk about this later." I ignored him.

And of course Linda was there, and of course I would see her the minute I walked in. She was arranged, rather prominently on display, in a fat armchair in the far corner. Sometime during the last year she'd learned how to sit—simply sit without doing a damned thing—and dominate a room. Boys surrounded her like fawning sycophants, brought her cokes and pretzels and potato chips, stood around waiting for a moment of her radiant attention while she sat like the princess in one of those silent movies set in some mythical Eastern European kingdom and accepted it all as perfectly normal. I was immediately sucked in, just as I always had been even when she'd been a gauche little kid, and walked across to her.

"Hello, John." I hadn't seen her since June, and she'd changed far more dramatically than I'd been prepared for. Her hair had lightened a shade, gone from taffy to a genuine blond, had become shorter too, was no longer fluffed into a bouffant but set into a carefully curled style. Her ears were hidden except for the lobes which were dotted with tiny pearls. She was wearing more makeup than I'd ever seen on her, a full *Vogue* production, and her nails were longer, filed into sharp ovals, and painted a brilliant scarlet. Her crackling cocktail dress, predictably blue, was nipped at the waist with a black leather belt; the full skirt was just slightly shorter than the current length to show off her magnificent legs in sleek champagne-colored stockings, shiny as glass, and on her tiny feet were the neatest sharpest highest French heels she'd been able to find in the most expensive little shop in Pittsburgh. It's too bad her mother hadn't let her read Freud (I thought with a mouthful of sour grapes); maybe then she'd understand what "over-compensation" meant.

She seemed to be with David Anderson—or maybe I should say he seemed to be with her; he was standing behind her chair stroking her hair. (Watch it, kid, I thought. Mess up her coiffure and she won't go out with you again.) With remarkable delicacy, he made some excuse and drifted away, leaving me alone with her; it was as though I'd brought a hurricane and plopped it down with the eye directly over Linda's chair, blowing all the other kids away like gulls. I stood looking down at her. The way she was sitting, the only appropriate position for me would be kneeling at her feet. Instead, I squatted on my heels like a garage mechanic about to slip the bill to the owner of a classy sports car; now our eyes were level. "How are you?" I said.

"I'm fine, John. How *are you?*"

I shrugged. "Doing all right." It was hard for me to see anyone I knew behind all that makeup. "You look stunning as usual."

She didn't smile. "Thank you . . . I wasn't sure you'd come tonight."

"Why not? I was invited." That seemed to have depleted our supply of words.

"Well," I said eventually, "you've sure got yourself a pretty boyfriend."

She didn't hesitate or change expression. "And you seem to be robbing the cradle again."

Oh you bitch, I thought. "What's that supposed to be, a joke?"

"If you want it to be a joke, it's a joke."

Now there was some human expression in the doll's face she'd painted onto herself—a clue in the narrowing of the eyes. I had, after all, known her a long time, and I saw that she was furious with me. Why? Because of Cassandra? I couldn't understand it.

"You've got your claws out tonight, kitten," I said.

"Meow, hiss," she said and made a scratching motion in the air with those sharp, shining red nails.

I tried to figure out what was going on. Although I hadn't seen her, I'd talked to her on the phone every few days all summer. Those calls had been like a barometer check on my own mental state—OK, boy, let's see if you can take it today—and I'd affected a distanced, detached, ironic tone that had become easier each time. I suppose I'd been needling her too. Something in me wanted to get a reaction out of her, some show of emotion that might tell me that she really had cared about me after all, and if I couldn't make her cry (I'd decided she didn't have any tears in her), then the least I could do was make her angry. But seeing her in the flesh, I couldn't go on with the show. I'd won, she was angry now, but it didn't feel like a victory. It felt as though our lives had tangled up into a knotty impasse. I couldn't forget her, and it hurt too much. I stood up to go.

"John," she said, glancing up at me quickly, giving something away.

"Yeah?"

"It was a joke . . . Forget it, OK?"

I sank down again into my squat. "Some joke."

"You started it."

"The hell I did." Although I knew that I had.

"Why are you always picking away at me? 'You've sure got yourself a pretty boyfriend.' What a thing to say."

"Let's call *that* a joke too, OK?"

"You don't have any right to say something like that to me."

"All right . . . Sure . . . I don't have any right."

She closed her eyes a moment, then looked directly into mine, shaking her head. Her mask had dropped away, and I knew her now, saw the pain and anger in her eyes. I couldn't understand what she thought I'd done to her. I hadn't been the one who'd ended it. I couldn't stand to look at her any longer. I stood up and walked away. When I glanced back from across the room, she was staring at the wall, her face closed. I went to look for Cassandra.

Cassy was doing all right. She was in the kitchen talking to some boys. One of them was David Anderson; as I walked in, she'd just made him laugh.

Revington grabbed me by the elbow and waltzed me out onto the back porch. "What the hell are you doing with Cassandra?" he said.

"It's none of your damned business, William."

"The hell it isn't. I introduced you into that house, remember? I feel responsible. Cassy's like a little sister to me. I remember her when she was twelve, for fuck's sake, and that's not very long ago either . . . What the hell's the matter with you, Dupre? You're doing it again. And it's not really fair. You could snow a little kid like that right out of her mind. Why don't you ever pick anybody old enough?"

"What did I do, William, beat you?"

He didn't answer. "To hell with you," I said and went back inside.

Strangely enough, the only person in that crowd who was pleasant to me that night was David Anderson. He was an absurdly handsome boy, an All-American Coca-Cola boy, almost too good to be true: six feet tall, suntanned and blond, a halfway decent miler, and a genuinely nice guy. (Even as jealous as I was, I managed to let myself like him.) His own guitar playing was at the ponk-CHINK stage; he sang Kingston Trio material in a muffled but pleasant tenor.

The party murmured and hummed along with him. He kept glancing over at me inquiringly: Would I play? Sure I'd play. I tuned up; my steel strings rang brilliantly against the memory of the muted thumping of his nylon ones.

The folk craze was so new in Raysburg that I don't think anybody had heard finger-picking except on records, but I'd spent the summer learning the rudiments of it, so a gratifying hush fell over the room. Nobody there might have liked me much, but they were ready to listen as they hadn't been to David, one of their own. About my voice there were, to put it kindly, certain problems. I hadn't been gifted with a mellifluous tenor suitable for Irish love ballads, had instead a harsh cracking strained bass. And perhaps (or so I told myself) the fact that I had so much trouble staying in tune was a blessing in disguise; it made me sing out forcefully, kept me from attempting melodic excursions that were beyond me. I worked over any song I was learning, at first note for note (playing the melody line on the guitar), then in slow motion, focusing my voice into the corner of my room. By the time I was ready to perform it in public, I would have sung the song hundreds of times, over-compensating, drilling the melody into my brain so I'd stay in tune no matter what else was happening—and I tried to get as much else happening as I could, turning each folk narrative into a tiny drama, trying to cover up the unpleasant timbre of my voice by hamming the words for all I was worth, singing *with character* I suppose I would have said.

My fingers, without much help from me, were picking

through the changes to "The House Carpenter." I looked around the room. I seemed to have gathered up everybody's attention (except for Linda's; she was staring away). David, expansively stretched over the couch, grinned and nodded to me; I imagine he was thinking that I was too shy to begin, but I wanted to see all of those kids, try to understand who they were.

Barbara Daniels, Sue Eberhardt, Linda Edmonds—all the girls in that crowd—dressed by steel money, protected, encircled, polished like lucent gems by steel money; country-club girls, Raysburg Cotillion girls, tennis and swimming-pool girls with their own private phones and their own cars, their lives continuous oil-smooth sailing over seas calmed by steel money. And just as their mothers had, they'd make lovely wives. That was the point, wasn't it? That was the point of *all of it*, wasn't it? The makeup and the enigmatic smiles, the high heels and the dresses, the breathy voices and lowered eyelashes, the flirting and kisses in shadows of immense safe houses, the game that tasted and smelled of sex, that never for a moment allowed me to forget my own clumsy sex, that drew me into a hall of mirrors, lost in reflections of reflections, images as stylized as any Geisha's, of girls who'd been curled, shaved, perfumed, powdered, painted, and immaculately costumed for these rites, like the work of a master jeweler requiring years of painstaking effort to fashion and perfect a setting for a gem that would remain invisible, that hot focus of sex that would remain inaccessible, because these girls were born to make lovely wives.

And here were the boyfriends, the clean-cut kids who'd grow up to be lawyers and businessmen and executives at Raysburg Steel, the modern knights who'd secure those lovely wives in immense safe houses with rolling lawns, and it would all go on forever to the soft shuffle of money being made, to the sound of chatty voices and tinkling laughter on the telephone, to the hiss of lawn sprinklers, the whir of lawn mowers, to the next generation of gems, of glittering daughters, going on forever in an America where it would always be two in the afternoon in mid-summer under sheepfleecy clouds in a bland blue sky— Like hell it would, I thought.

I don't know how I could have known it then, but I did—that it couldn't be allowed to go on forever, that it had to be cracked right open, the exquisitely smooth porcelain surface broken to reveal the addled yolk underneath, and when it happened, the stink would be like something that had been rotting for a thousand years.

I looked at everyone in the room, came at last to Cassandra. She wasn't like those other girls, and I knew it. I looked into her wonderfully direct eyes and began to sing:

> Well met, well met, my own true love.
> Well met, well met, cried he.
> I've just returned from the salt salt sea,
> All for the love of thee.

I'd sung just this way for Linda, sending a song directly to her, saying with my eyes: this is for *you*. Linda had always lowered her lashes; the blood had always risen slowly into her cheeks, but Cassy winked at me, and, smiling wickedly, joined me in the second verse in a voice as clear and easy as a boy soprano's. I'd never heard Cassandra sing before, and the sound of her struck at the music inside me.

We were coming to the girl's verse, her answer to the man "just returned from the salt salt sea." I gave Cassandra a nod, hoping she'd understand and sing alone if I dropped out, and she did it!

> Well, if you could have married the
>   king's daughter dear,
> I'm sure you are to blame.
> For I am married to a house carpenter,
> Find him a nice young man.

She pronounced "nice young man" with a drawling downstate accent, winked at me again, and drew laughs (particularly from David Anderson who fell back onto the couch laughing). Cassandra and I sang together:

> She fitted on her rich attire
> So glorious to behold,
> And as she walked along her way,
> She shone like the glittering gold.

When we finished, they actually applauded us.

Now I see that party as having taken place on some crucial dividing line; something new was going on that I don't think could have been possible even a year earlier. Cassandra with her lean adolescent figure, in a boy's cotton shirt, blue jeans and penny loafers, her hair in need of washing and not a touch of makeup on her face, was immediately at a curious advantage over all those other girls in their nylons and heels. What I'd predicted for her turned out to be true: by the time she was sixteen, the boys were after her by the dozen.

Linda did all right too, following on the path she'd already chosen. Her friends teased her for being a clothes horse, but she was listed as "most popular girl" in her year book, and she was Homecoming Queen, so it worked. But gradually her time was fading out and Cassandra's was coming in. Sue Eberhardt told Barbara Daniels who told Revington who told me that Linda really wanted David Anderson. But who was he dating by spring, who did he take to the Senior Prom, who did he think he wanted to marry, and who finally broke his heart? It was Cassandra.

I can't blame Cassy for not being more generous; she didn't know that anything was changing (none of us did). When I took her home after the party that night, she said, "So that was the famous Linda Edmonds, huh? Whew, what a bitch."

LYLE WAS having a tumultuous summer too. Our last stop before going home to bed was always the back room of the Pines. It was as black as the bottom of a mine shaft in there, and we'd be surrounded by sad old drunks, the crapped-out derelicts of the end of night. From our booth we could watch the dim uneasy silhouettes of the customers lined up as they waited to climb the narrow stairs to the whorehouse above the bar. Most of the hooded candles on the tables would have gone out by then, and a harsh yellow glare from a small window leading to the kitchen glowed like one of those eerie glimpses of a hellish other world in a Bosch painting. We'd order spaghetti and meatballs, and eventually two plates would come sliding through that fiery hole, be carried to our table by the waitress whose face we couldn't see in the dark; she'd also bring us two mason jars, one full of powdered cheese, the other full of ground dry chilies. We'd order more whiskey with water for a chaser; strangely enough, they wouldn't sell us beer because it was after hours. Now I remember an ambience of excitement and danger as though our adolescent speculations were as complex and potent as the Cabala. Lyle's face would be lost in dim shadow, his long bony hands bright as they made passes over the candle, as he gestured in the smoky air, clutching his pipe that was always going out, his eyes glittering as he told me: "We need more Christs, more Buddhas. We need more Leonardos . . . I want to combine the precision of a scientist with the passion of an artist."

At least that's the way I remember it, but more than likely it was an ordinary enough bar and we supplied the demonic background ourselves. Even though I was having a wonderful time with Cassandra, I couldn't forget Linda, and I couldn't shake the hollow ache inside me or the old voice I thought should have fallen silent by then, the one that kept saying: "You may be enjoying yourself at the moment, but it won't last. You're never going to be happy in your life—because you're not *a real boy.*"

And Lyle was intentionally going mad; I'd given him the idea. It had been all the way back in our sophomore year when we'd first been getting to know each other. We'd been milling around and talking, waiting for the bell that would signal the official beginning of the school day, and I told Lyle that I wanted to go mad. As was true with most of my pronouncements then, I was only partially serious. Lyle reacted deadpan, as though I'd casually remarked that I was planning to go to Europe some day. I think I said it primarily to shock him; his lack of shock goaded me on to elaborate. "Normal experience isn't enough," I said. "We must also experience madness to develop the potentials of our personalities."

He giggled nervously. I could see that I'd got him. "My God," he said, "how are you going to go mad?"

"Stop sleeping, stop eating, move continually, drink constantly, dance, listen to music . . . until something in me short-circuits and I'm suddenly outside."

The more I talked, the more I liked the idea. As a child, I'd wanted to know what it was like to be shocked, so with my hands dripping wet, I'd played with the light switches and electrical plugs—doing everything I'd been told I must not do. I got shocked. I'm sure that I saw, briefly, the blue flame of the charge. I cried, and my mother comforted me and scolded me at the same time: "I told you that you'd get shocked." Even as I was crying, I felt annoyed with her for not understanding. I had wanted to know what it was like— and now I *knew*. "That's what I mean," I told Lyle. "*Experience,* even if it hurts."

I talked on about it until the bell rang, filled in more details, as Lyle stared at me, fascinated. I didn't realize how capable he was of taking any idea seriously and trying it out. Just after the bell rang, he looked back with a laugh and said, "I think you're mad already."

But now, that summer after we graduated, he was telling me: "You were right. Normal experience isn't enough."

He'd been running to keep himself in shape for cross-country in the fall, but he gradually abandoned it. He'd found more important things and was doing all of his running in his mind. He would read all day, drink every night, and walk the streets until dawn; every once in a while he dropped in to St. Stans to chat it all over with his parish priest. I began to hear more about this shadowy figure Lyle had always referred to before simply as "my priest" or "my confessor." The man began to develop a distinct personality in my imagination, although I'd never met him. He was an old man who'd come over from Poland and used to brag that he could say Mass faster than any other priest in the Ohio Valley. He said he'd never die until the last of the immigrants of his own generation died ahead of him. And I gathered that the priest was forming an impression of me too. "He thinks you're the Antichrist himself," Lyle told me, giggling. I imagined the old man as some ignorant and narrowly fanatic Savonarola.

Lyle had decided that science and religion had separated during the Renaissance and that *he* was the one who was going to put them back together in one vast schema that would encompass the universe. "I don't want to specialize. I want to know *everything*." He read orthodox writers, starting with Saint Augustine, but he also began to stray from the straight and narrow. The puzzled librarian at the public library had to order dozens of obscure books for him from Pittsburgh. He read the Apocrypha so that he could decide for himself if they should have been excluded from the Bible. His priest said he was on dangerous ground. "You don't know everything," Lyle told him.

Lyle worked his way through Church history, finding points of doctrine in various councils where he was sure the Church had made the wrong turn—took those arguments back to his priest. The poor man was having a hard time keeping up. "He doesn't know anything about the Lateran Councils," Lyle told me gleefully. "He wants to send me to the Jesuits." Working his way through the complicated history of the Reformation, Lyle concluded that Luther had been right, that the Church should have been reformed then and there and Luther kept inside it. Lyle read about the Inquisition and became indignant; he read Giordano Bruno, said, "*There* was a man who had the answer, and they burned him." At the same time he was reading about Einstein, modern physics, relativity theory. He'd found a name for what he was doing. "I'm going to work out a unified field theory of the universe . . . put science and ethics back together. They never should have been separated in the first place." When he read about Pascal's fiery transforming vision, he knew that he had to experience the same thing himself. "Our scientific knowledge is like a many-sided polygon," he said, "and God is a circle. We can keep adding sides to the polygon, and it will grow closer to the circle, but it will never *become* the circle. Except by a leap. I want to make that leap."

Lyle's insomnia this time around had nothing to do with running. At first it had been hard, he said, a rigorous spiritual discipline, to go without sleep, but, by the Grace of the Holy Spirit, the need to sleep had been lifted from him. He was fasting too, and praying at dawn on the banks of the Ohio River, but he kept on drinking with me, using me as a sounding board for his ideas. One night, at dawn, my doorbell rang. I woke immediately, knew what it had to be, jumped up and ran downstairs fast. My father, with all his nightly whiskey under his belt, could sleep through anything, but I heard my mother call out querulously: "What is it, John? What's the matter?"

"Don't worry. It's nothing. Go back to sleep." I opened the door, and there was Lyle. He was shaking all over; his teeth were chattering. He couldn't say a word.

I thought the occasion warranted a raid on the old man's liquor cabinet, so carried a bottle of Jim Beam and a couple glasses up to my room. Lyle still hadn't spoken, and, even though there was a hot sun rising, he looked as though he was freezing to death. I gave him a blanket. He wrapped himself in it and sat on the edge of my bed. Sweat was pouring down his face. "What's the matter, boy?"

He shook his head. I gave him a shot of whiskey. He drank it. "I saw something," he said.

"What?"

"On the banks of the river. I was sitting on the banks of the river. I saw it."

"What?"

He'd begun to shake again, so badly that I had to take the glass from his hand. "Just like in the Bible, John. Just like all the saints. Just like Pascal. I had a vision. I saw it."

"All right. What was it?"

"Hell . . . I saw hell. I understand everything now. I know what's happened. Everything stinks too much, and God's run away from this mess. Hell's right here. It's the Devil's world."

I DIDN'T see Lyle for a couple weeks after that. His parents wouldn't let me talk to him when I phoned, and he never called me back. I went down to his place and bounced a pebble off his window—our old middle-of-the-night trick—but nothing happened. Then, early one afternoon, he turned up. He had a fresh haircut, was wearing pressed slacks and a sports jacket. He smiled shyly. "I've come to say goodbye," he said.

"Why goodbye?" I said. "We've got three weeks to go."

"I'm leaving early." He'd applied to half a dozen colleges, been accepted by most of them, and had chosen the University of California—the farthest one from Raysburg. "It's time to put all this behind me."

He told me that after his vision, he'd come first to me, and then had gone straight to the church. He wouldn't tell me what he'd said to the priest or the priest to him. He claimed that they'd spoken in Polish, but I didn't believe it. I was pretty sure that Lyle didn't know much more than twenty words of Polish. All he would say was: "He showed me the way to peace." And then he went home and went to bed; he slept for two days. When he got up, he began to pack for school. "Greater minds than mine have thought about these things, John. I'm not going to do it anymore." He sounded as though he was reciting from a catechism.

I sat and looked at him: my oldest, best friend. I could already sense what was happening, and I knew that if he didn't leave soon, I'd begin to cry. "I committed the sin of pride," he said. "I wanted God to show me His face." He left for California the next day, and he has never, to my knowledge, come back to Raysburg.

Remembering Lyle's conviction that he'd been cursed, I think now that he knew something sooner than I did: we had *all* been cursed. Along with our fervor and passion, our drive and excitement, there was something else in our lives that was excessive and dangerous. No adult we knew could teach us anything. Our parents were ordinary people struggling with ordinary problems; they didn't have much to offer beyond common-sense advice on how to make it as easy as possible for ourselves in the world, and we didn't want to make it easy. We wanted *truth*. Nobody had much to say about that. We had a teacher or two in school who did something more than put in his time and draw a salary, and we did enjoy seeing adults who could still be excited by the Glory of Greece or the Periodic Table of the Elements, but none of them was concerned with the Socratic question of how to live, and I don't think we would have accepted advice from them even if they had been; the classroom was too far from life. Because our religion centered around athletics, I think we might have listened to our coaches if they'd been anything more than little boys in men's bodies. But all we had were books and each other. Looking back, I think that wasn't enough.

It's easy to make the mistake of nostalgia, to remember those days as an endless sunrise and forget the pain and confusion. But running through that time *was* a constant thread of greatness, because, I think, things were happening, constantly, and we were changing, constantly, and what we wanted appeared to be just one step ahead of us for the taking: it was only a matter of developing the skill, the courage, and the stamina to reach out and take it. Our creed was "experience and suffering." That is what we wanted. And that is what we were to get.

IT SEEMS that every historian must remind us that historical periods are arbitrary, that they fade into each other imperceptibly, that we cannot pin down a date and say, "this is when it began," or "this is when it ended." But then, after we have been warned, we must always be given a specific date of some specific event, for, of course, that's what we wanted all along: the sharp pin to poke into that imperceptible flow of time and say, "Here!"—a confluence of strands, a nexus of symbols, arbitrary to some degree, but resonant and easy to remember.

One afternoon in the late-summer Raysburg dog days,

Cassandra and I were walking along the river bank. I was telling her about running. Well, I suppose what I was doing was bragging. In the male world of athletics, I couldn't have gotten away with it; someone would have asked me how many meets I'd placed in, what my best times were, and the game would have been over. It's true that I'd come an astonishing way in three years, but placing *fifth* in one meet and averaging six minutes a mile in training didn't exactly make me a Herb Elliott. But I thought I could impress Cassandra; my stories had always impressed Linda. In fact, she used to time me. We'd meet at the school track, me in my shorts and sneakers and she in sandals and a pretty summer dress (because she knew what I liked), and she'd arrange herself carefully under a tree in the shade where the sun wouldn't poison her delicate skin, and she'd hold the stopwatch and smile at me each time I passed in those eight laps that make up two miles. Linda had always seemed *very* impressed. But Cassandra said, "I'm a pretty good runner too, you know."

"Oh, are you?" I remember clearly that I thought I was humoring her.

"Yeah. When I was twelve, there wasn't a single boy my own age who could catch me. Some of the big kids could . . . but not a single boy my own age . . . We used to have races."

Cassandra had a quality about her then—I suppose "childlike" is the word to use, but the child she was like was a fierce undomesticated child. She'd described herself to me as "a little alley cat." Until she'd turned thirteen, she'd played with the boys in the neighborhood (stick ball, softball, kick the can), and the air of that time still clung to her—a separate society, closed subculture, the back-alley boys, intense preteens with their own demands and a code as bleak and honorable as Hemingway's, tolerating the adult world ("the big people," Cassandra still called them) in precisely the way an independent cat tolerates his owners. I didn't know what to make of this; I was more comfortable with the daughter of the Raysburg Liberal, the reader, the bright girl recently grown into "Cassandra" than I was with a kid called "Cassy" just a year away from being an alley cat. There was little that could have prepared me; Linda had been childlike too at times, but her version had been a baby doll, a sex kitten. It would take Cassandra a few more years to learn to use her sex as a weapon, and Linda seemed always to have known how.

The day was immensely thick and hot with that steambath oppression of West Virginia in August. We were looking out over the Ohio River; the sun reflected there burned behind my eyelids, heating the retinae, the world as a red haze pressing in even when I closed my eyes, dizzying: the huge size of that afternoon. The pupils of Cassandra's eyes were contracted to points, leaving gray discs, translucent as marbles but flickering with energy—the live eye. Her entire face was tensed against a sun so bright that it brought us up into clear focus—the vivid irritability of living tissue. No way we could miss it with the vibrant small muscles of the face in motion, with the blood showing under the skin, blue lines, pink flush, with sweat on the forehead and sweat between the thighs. I could stretch out in this heat, extend myself, soak it up into me until I was hot to the bone. I didn't know yet what I had. I didn't know in my guts that I wouldn't be eighteen forever.

She took off, exploding into movement like a flushed grouse. "Catch me, John!"

So fast that she was already ten yards away, sprinting along the path, before I began to move. I think that I must have laughed. I took off after her, not all-out by any means, but with the pace I would have used for a moderate 440. I'd trained at this for three years. I'd been running all summer. I hadn't started smoking yet. Weeks of grieving over Linda had killed my appetite, and my weight had dropped to a hundred and thirty-seven. I knew that I'd never been as fit in my life. (But I didn't know that I'd never be that fit again.)

We ran about fifty yards, and she was still moving away from me. I was used to running flat cinder tracks, and she was much better than I was at bounding around stones and through brush. She was all out, sprinting like a dash man. She'll kill herself in this heat, I thought. She'll drop like a stone. I'll just keep a moderate pace, and I'll catch her when she starts to tie up.

But by the time I saw that she'd begun to slow down, she must have been a hundred yards ahead of me. I stretched out my stride, moving into the pace I reserved for the end of races. I was sure that when I caught her, it would be the end: she would have destroyed herself. "Hey," I yelled after her, "I'm a *distance* man, not a *sprinter.*" She'd slowed almost to a walk, but when she heard me, she took off again. I saw that for a moment she'd pressed her hand hard into her side,

144

squeezing herself just below the ribs on the right. Yeah, I thought, there it is: the knife in the guts. She's done. And I began to sprint.

Running regularly, you learn a sense of pace and distance, and I knew that we'd covered about a half mile. As far as I was concerned, she'd made her point; any girl who could run a half mile in that heat, at that pace, was welcome to my respect and praise. But now I just wanted it to be over; it had stopped being fun, and I was working. My mouth was drying out in that horribly familiar way I knew from track practice on hot days. Sweat was burning my eyes so badly that I stripped my shirt off and mopped my face. I let my form go to hell (Lyle wasn't around to see it) and pushed myself until I caught up to her. "Yeah, you really can run," I said, or something like it. But instead of stopping as I'd expected her to, she kept on going. She didn't run like a girl, no swivel at the hips, no flopping about with the arms like a wounded sparrow. She ran with her knees close together and her feet pointed straight ahead, with a long economical stride, her white shoes—those silly little tennis shoes with the sharply pointed toes that girls wore in those days—flashing in the sun. I fell into her rhythm, and we ran along side by side, over an open grassy stretch now. We'd been at it for nearly a mile, and I was sure she'd quit soon. "You're great," I said, hoping that would satisfy her. But she kept on going. She had a perfect stride for a distance runner: level, simple, and efficient.

We hit brush again, and she bounded off ahead of me. I threw away my shirt which I'd been carrying balled up in my hand, clenched my fists, and dug in to follow her. She'd set her hair that morning, but now the curl was falling out; her blouse was as wet as if she'd been swimming in it; there was even sweat pouring down her shaved legs, making them gleam in the sun as though they'd been burnished. We'd covered a mile in something like seven minutes and were moving into the second one. I let myself sink into the mindless, gut-it-out slogging of the middle of a race, glad I was wearing Bermudas and not jeans, sneakers and not my heavy engineer boots. Sweat had spattered the lenses of my glasses until I couldn't see; I took them off and thrust them into a side pocket. We broke out of brush and into a clear area next to railroad tracks, and I pulled up alongside her again.

She glanced over at me. She was panting like a dog, but she managed to say, "That's not fair . . . I can't . . . take off . . . *my* shirt."

"It's too hot for this," I said.

She didn't answer. She kept on running.

It *was* too hot for it. I was beginning to feel light, stunned, and dizzy, the first twist of nausea in my belly, that familiar gut full of stones that you can never learn how to live with. I knew that she had to be suffering. Anybody who didn't train regularly would have been suffering. And I no longer cared about whether I beat her or she beat me. Now I just wanted to know how long we could keep it up.

After the second mile, something lifted, and I felt light and easy. We thought in those days that trained runners were not supposed to get a second wind, but I was getting one, as

146

though I'd run through a deep bog, and out of it, onto clear grass. I don't think either of us was doing it intentionally, but we were matching each other stride for stride. She glanced over at me and grinned. I grinned back. We didn't have to say a thing. The Ohio River was unrolling on our left, the sun above us was high and fat, the dazzling reality behind thousands of years of icons: the smile, the open hands at the end of each carefully drawn beam. We're not usually given the insight to know when we're running through the core of our life; usually it's years later when we look back and say, "Oh!" But I was lucky enough to know it, and hope, when I'm dying, I'll be lucky enough to remember it. The rhythm of running moves like the heartbeat, first one foot and then the other, like the pulse, deep thrust out, kick back of the veins, the twin beat that is music before there was music, *löpar-glädje* the Scandinavian distance runners called it, translates into English as "the joy of running," but it means life.

That clear and opened space could not last forever. We must have covered most of the third mile. We exchanged a glance that said it: Yeah, we really *do* have to stop. "To that tree?" I said, pointing. She didn't answer, but she began to sprint.

I no longer wanted to beat her. But I didn't want her to beat me either. As clearly as I can remember it, I think that I *might* have been able to pull just ahead of her over those last few yards. But I don't know for sure. All I know is that we passed the tree side by side. She threw herself down onto the grass, and I yelled at her, "Get up!" I didn't have enough breath to explain, tell her that she might pass out if she didn't keep walking. I grabbed her by one hand, dragged her to her feet, and pulled her along with me, stumbling. My entire field of vision was contracting, then exploding, with my heart beat. After a moment I let go of her hand, leaned against a tree, and threw up.

I heard a sympathetic splashing sound, looked up and saw that she was trying to smile at me with the vomit still running down her chin. "Oh, Jesus, Cassandra," I said, "have you ever thought of training for the Olympics?"

She didn't seem to be able to speak yet. She peeled off her sneakers. She hadn't been wearing socks, and the little toes of both her feet were worn bloody. "These goddamned shoes," she said, still gasping for breath, and threw them into the river. One at a time. Carefully. They spun over and over whitely in the sun and fell with a splash.

We began walking back the way we had come. "I love you, Cassandra," I said.

"That's all right, John Dupre . . . as long as you're not *in love* with me." I didn't answer. We continued to stumble along. We must have looked like a couple plague victims.

But my happiness was complete; nothing could shadow it. "Do you know what I mean?" she said. "*In love* is going steady and tying people down and all that crap . . . *Love* is just . . . love."

"I understand . . . Yeah, I do . . . I love you, Cassandra."

"I love you too, John."

The Fifties were over.

Author's Afterword

The *Difficulty at the Beginning* quartet does not fit easily into any simple category of writing. It is partially based upon two of my previously published novels (*The Knife in My Hands* and *Cutting Through*), but it is also partially based upon even earlier writing that never made it into those novels, and much of the writing is new. Although my main character, John Dupre, feels to me like the same person he always was, I have massively restructured his story. I consider *The Knife in My Hands* and *Cutting Through* to be simply two of nearly a dozen early preliminary drafts and *Difficulty at the Beginning*, in its current form, the final draft. Taken as a whole, the quartet is far more of a new work than it is a revision.

When I first conceived of this writing project in Boston in 1969, I called it *Difficulty at the Beginning*. By the time I began working with Ed Carson at General Publishing in the late 1970s, I had, under that title, amassed over a thousand pages of writing and notes. From that material I extracted four short linked novels; they comprised a classic *Bildungsroman* covering twelve crucial years in the life of John Dupre (sixteen to twenty-eight) and in the life of North Americans generally (that period of immense social and political change, 1958–1970). For convenience of publication, we dropped my original title, and the four short novels were divided equally between two volumes: *The Knife in My Hands* and *Cutting Through*. I was suffering from a number of personal problems while I was attempting to complete those books; I gradually lost the essential internal compass that keeps writers honest, and what I managed to do was far from my best work. When I finished *Cutting Through*, writer's block shut me down, and I didn't write again for nearly two years.

Twenty years later, when I was considering the republication of my early novels, I had another look at *The Knife in*

My Hands and *Cutting Through*—the only books of mine that had always felt incomplete to me, as though I had abandoned them before they were ready. Just as I had suspected, they contained some of the best writing I had ever done in my life and some of the worst. I certainly didn't want them reissued the way they were, but I felt that mere revision was out of the question. I knew that if I wanted to get John Dupre's story right this time, I would have to go back to where I'd started—not merely to the two published books, but back to the story itself.

I began by reading the earliest drafts, now conveniently housed and neatly catalogued in the archives at the University of British Columbia Library. In some cases, I was reading material I hadn't seen in thirty years. I can't say that I felt as distant from it as though it had been written by someone else; it affected me deeply, but exactly how it affected me is difficult to describe. The younger author was capable of some extraordinarily sloppy, silly, and overwrought passages; he also wrote with an enviable lack of restraint—the swashbuckling élan of an unpublished writer with nothing to lose. I incorporated some of his work into my current work. He's learned a lot from me over the years, but recently I've learned a lot from him too.

John Dupre's story came vividly to life for me once again, and I assembled a skeleton framework of it which contained writing from both the earlier drafts and the published version; I then worked through it, rewriting and adding new material as necessary. The further I went into this project, the more new writing I had to do. Eventually a new ending emerged, one that I had never imagined before; as I worked my way toward it, I found nothing usable left from any earlier version. In the final two books of the quartet, nearly all of the writing is new.

Of the four books of *Difficulty at the Beginning, Running*

is the only one that is not radically different from the previously published version. Readers who remember the first half of *The Knife in My Hands* will see that what appears here is much the same story, but I have changed many small details—trimmed away minor threads that led nowhere, added a few pages of entirely new material, and (if I have succeeded in doing what I set out to do) altered the overall feeling of the book in a subtle but significant way.

I have tried to be true to the voice (or *voices*—the four books have different styles) of the younger writer I used to be, but I felt no compulsion to reproduce his occasional vagueness, clumsiness, purple prose, or solecisms. And I have tried to be true to John Dupre and his times. In a jacket blurb he kindly wrote for *The Knife in My Hands*, Robert Kroetsch called that book "a real autobiography of a fictional character," a phrase that pleased me then and still pleases me today because I see it as a neat and accurate description of what I set out to do so many years ago. John's story was one I needed to tell. I didn't get it right the first time; I've had another go at it. This is probably going to sound distinctly odd, but—from my subjective experience inside my writing life—the story exists independently of me, has gone on, and will continue to go on, however I write about it or *whether* I write about it. In going back to that story, I was not free to write anything I wanted. John is far more my Rabbit Angstrom than he is my Sal Paradise and, insofar as his story is also social history, I am less an author than a chronicler.

I consider the quartet to be essential to my writing—the nucleus from which radiate all of the themes I explore in other books. Only time, of course, will judge literary merit, but to me, the author, *Difficulty at the Beginning* feels like the core of my literary life.

Keith Maillard, Vancouver, May 14, 2005

The *Difficulty at the Beginning* quartet follows John Dupre from his awkward high-school years in the late 1950s through the burgeoning counterculture movement of the early 1960s to the tumultuous and devastating late-1960s political and psychedelic underground.

Each of the four volumes is written in the style of the times. In *Running* the façade of post-WWII American optimism is just beginning to crack. *Morgantown* hums and throbs with the freewheeling energy and free-floating angst of youth pushing against the boundaries of social acceptability. *Lyndon Johnson and the Majorettes* situates the anxiety of the years following Kennedy's assassination and the impending threat of the Vietnam draft in the oppressive heat of a West Virginia summer. In the final volume, *Looking Good,* all the currents of the high sixties draw together in an explosive climax.

By any measure, *Difficulty at the Beginning* is a major addition to American and Canadian literature, a brilliant and supremely readable social chronicle that ranks with the best of North American fiction.

MORGANTOWN • 1-897142-07-2 • FEBRUARY 2006

LYNDON JOHNSON AND THE MAJORETTES • 1-897142-08-0 • APRIL 2006

LOOKING GOOD • 1-897142-09-9 • SEPTEMBER 2006

BOOKS BY KEITH MAILLARD

Novels

Two Strand River (1976)

Alex Driving South (1980)

The Knife in My Hands (1981)

Cutting Through (1982)

Motet (1989)

Light in the Company of Women (1993)

Hazard Zones (1995)

Gloria (1999)

The Clarinet Polka (2002)

Difficulty at the Beginning

       Book 1: *Running* (2005)

       Book 2: *Morgantown* (2006)

       Book 3: *Lyndon Johnson and the Majorettes* (2006)

       Book 4: *Looking Good* (2006)

Poetry

Dementia Americana (1995)